graham greig

BAT TORPOR

graham greig - poet, novelist, and non-conformist - was born in Possilpark, Glasgow, 1956, and now resides in East Whitburn, a.k.a. The Bash. After starting his working life as a butcher in the early 1970s he subsequently found employment as a spray-painter, warehouseman, administrator, and hotelier. His first novel, *Neddie And Hess*, appeared in 2013. He has since published a number of volumes of poetry, a play and a further five novels.

PROOF

NOVELS BY GRAHAM GREIG

A Better Serial Than Breakfast

Pamphleteer: a shorts novel

Filename Fastkill

Exploration D

Stalin's Left Arm

Bat Torpor

*

****

BAT TORPOR

****

*

graham greig

© 2024 by graham greig

All rights reserved. No part of this book may be reproduced, stored in a retrieval system or transmitted in any form or by any means without the prior written permission of the author, except by a reviewer who may quote brief passages in a review to be printed in a newspaper, magazine, or journal.

The author asserts the moral right to be identified as the author of this work.

ISBN 9798328556057

Set in Times New Roman.

This is a work of fiction, one man's vision of things. No correspondence between the people, places, and events in the real world is intended. What correspondence might exist is purely the result of coincidence.

g.g.

I advice you to remain uniformly quiescent and above all activity. Do not deceive yourselves with conceptual thinking, and do not look anywhere for the truth, for all that is needed is to refrain from allowing concepts to arise.

       Huang Po

Bat Torpor

No. 22
The b job, sugar-free, death machine

As they lingered by domestic a moment or two, scavengers on the fringe, hunters of inappropriate elation, their strange apparel riding up at the crotch, Ellis made discreet inquiries as to the health of Joyce, knowing only too well that her breast reduction had been a complete success, leaving her with the handful she'd so desired rather than the devil's dumplings she'd been plagued with since her teens.
 "Well, she's up and about again," answered Simon as he lifted a trick from the centre of the table: "Four ... Hate to see her down so long." Billy smiled and shook his head. "Well, I suppose it keeps her occupied and out from under our feet. Acts like a lunatic at times if you ask me, with all her harebrained schemes for this that and the next thing. Remember that last idea took her fancy? ... What the hell was it again?"
 Ellis stood and made for the bar. He'd decided, much against his better judgement, to ask her out. That way, he reasoned, if a refusal were delivered it wouldn't weigh so heavy as it would if he were to return to the table, long faced and on edge. His friends awaiting his return.
 He walked as slow as possible, building courage, until he was able to go no further.

**

Outside in the cool light of day the sun shone watery, and he punched the air, jubilant at having secured a date. He was revitalised ... Alive ... The tightly wound coil that had been himself these last weeks was now slowly dissipating, and in the pallid November light all was ablaze: colours he hadn't seen in an age jumped at him, and with each step along Grand Street his confidence grew.

He acknowledged those he knew in passing, where for the last while he'd been more inclined to wander aimlessly with his head bowed to the ground, tired and unenthusiastic to the point of disbelief. He'd been after Joyce for as long as he could recall, and now she was finally his he felt good. It didn't bother him in the slightest she was of a different persuasion than himself, and along with the various stories he'd heard circulating among the boys in the bar of how she was into transvestites - rubber, PVC, leather, wetlook, directoire, frilly, pretty, plastic, playsuit, waspies, French - and a whole host of other similarly outrageous activities commencing after dark, he didn't let it worry him. It only served to strengthen his resolve and he was quite glad - after the event - he'd got round to asking her out: tomorrow was her day off and she'd agreed to have him pick her up at home and take her out to the coast, provided the weather held. However, not having transport of his own due to a ban sustained for being under the influence he'd have to borrow his brother-in-law's. It hadn't been a problem in the past, and if it was in perfect working order and Neil didn't need it for anything important that day, everything would be fine. He'd have to put petrol in it of course, that was only natural. After all, a car for the coast was a car for the coast and filling it with fuel was obligatory.

**

Clarion and a clash of cymbals.

A cloaked and hooded figure takes to the podium, centre stage, filling the air with gasconade.

Grand Wizard Racehate: "All nigras is trash ... and as such should be swept to the sea." Crosses are burnt, shotguns pumped to the void. His pestiferous speech persists.

"... and when the sea is full, they should be ploughed ... ploughed to the land as fertiliser, for they ain't nothing 'cept shit, and that's where shit belongs ... in the ground ... Ain't no room for mixed marriages here."

A youth, uninvited, believing a concert in progress wanders mistakenly into the arena. All heads gyrate.

"You! ... Boy! ... At the back!"

"Me?"

"Yea you ... You got an opinion?"

"Opinion?"

"Yea, nigras boy ... You got an opinion about nigras?"

The youth, thinking he'd left this sort of sickening bigotry behind looks at the Wizard in amazement.

"Well, you see," he answers. "Where I come from in the central belt a mixed marriage is between two whites and the ignant mothers that mix it there are as dumb as you poor fucks, with their NO SURRENDER and UP THE IRA."

**

He'd lain awake most of the night and what sleep he did manage to catch was interspersed with strange and often alarming dreams.
  They left first thing in the morning for the coast.

**

Waves that rolled straight in from the sea and rushed in foaming over the land till they were broken up into circles of froth lapped their soles as they walked in the natural contour the beach at Contraband Cove, flotsam and jetsam littering their path: knotted Durex collapsed in on themselves, milky liquid pasting them flat, come and go with the flow. A buoy ... A length of rope ... Crates thrown overboard by a job-weary purser far away at sea, bleached and dried by the salt and sun lie at the mouth of a cave, pushed up long ago when a higher tide marked the shoreline. Assorted bottles, plastic and glass, their labels peeled or illegible were caught between rocks in pools of life as the sea receded back on itself. Crisp bags, bread wrappers, a mixture of branches from god knows where, toilet paper (disintegrating), myriad drinks cans, bloodied sanitary towels (medium, regular, and heavy), a selection of odd footwear and the hull of an old fishing boat.
  They walked in silence, the breeze from the sea sweeping their bodies with a shivering intensity, until finally Ellis suggested they go to the cave

they'd passed for a smoke and a bit of shelter. Joyce said yes, then quickly broke off, running to its mouth before disappearing inside where the remnants of a once glowing fire lay sodden in the sand. Ellis was in at her back.

"Soon have that going again," he said, pointing to the pile of charcoaled waste lying on the ground in front of him. "I'll go see what I can find to start it and we'll be warmer than hell in no time."

She slumped hard against the wall and blew a billowing plume of breath and smoke to the void. "For heaven's sake Jeff hurry up," she said. "It's as cold in here." She was rubbing her hands together to gain body heat, her cheeks red on pearly skin.

He was back in five minutes and within fifteen the entire cave was aglow, their shadows dancing apparitions on the wall as they knelt together to smoke another cigarette on top of the coat he'd spread in front of the naked flames.

This was his opportunity. And if half the stories he'd heard were to be believed it had to be now. He put his arm around her, caressed her shoulders then kissed her softly on the lips. She responded in kind and before he knew what was happening, they'd both fallen retrogress to the ground, she on top, skirt riding upward.

They kissed with tongues deep in throat, wriggling like slippery combatants in a pit of slime, until finally opening his shirt she went down, loosening his Levi's at the waist to free nine inches of throbbing flesh, straight and hard. A viscid bead of clear liquid was hanging precariously from its eye, and she licked with the tip of her tongue, slowly bringing it back into her mouth before the serious business of fellatio proper began. She licked his scrotum, sucking each ball individually and it took all his powers of self-control to fight the urge to come. She lingered an eternity, licking, and sucking, biting, and teasing, until finally rimming him she made her way up his distended penis in the churning motion of counterfeit coition: JHUTHAMETHUNA!

She sucked hard, working the base of his shaft with her long slender fingers, moaning sexually in time with her evenly spaced strokes. Never in his life had he witnessed such an accomplished head, and all the other pricks she'd serviced only served as a timer in blowing his tubes. He arched his back forcing his penis deep into her gobbling mouth, great torrents of jism hitting the back of her throat. He arched again ... A second volley. This time forcing it deeper as she swallowed in quick succession his salty come, her fingers milking his every drop: drained.

**

Fieldtreepyloncottagesea BOOM! Phantom in hot pursuit, Mig on the run. Burst of gunfire: Cak cak cak cak cak cak cak. Miss. WHOOSH! "Next time bastard." In again on its tail, sights centred for the kill. Land-to-air in the undercarriage, direct hit, phantom down, puff of smoke. No. 2: In from the east, sun low: Cak cak cak cak cak cak cak. Mig banks left avoids strike, turns on phantom with zap zap missiles. Two down one to go. "Fucker!"

Straight from the centre of a cloud formation, head-to-head. Cak cak cak cak cak cak cak. Zap! Zap! WHOOSH! Simultaneous obliteration. Blank. Flashing screen: £1:00 per play ... £1:00 per play ... £1:00 per play ...

Inside the booth, Joyce had straddled and was facing him, her stockings rent from the afternoon's pleasures, skirt high, her mound protruding like the bonnet of a VW beetle.

"Almost as quick as yourself," she joked, suggestively toying the lobe of his ear as a cat gamed a fly before devouring it like a tidbit. He pulled her head forward with the palm of his hand from the rear and kissed her lips; those self-same cherry lips that an hour before had been licking his rectum and sucking hard on his erect member in a way known only to a select few and perchance the men's rugby team, fishing club and the regulars at the Pit where she worked.

"Excuse me, can I have a go?"

A boy aged eight or nine was standing in the mouth of The Death Machine awaiting his chance to take control of the aircraft in the hope of becoming ACE.

"Sorry kid," said Joyce. "We're leaving." She climbed off and out, and the front when they broke the arcade was peaceful.

**

It was November and not many people were inclined to take to the coast at that time of year for fear of the bitter cold wind which blew unhindered in from the sea. A small harbour to their left was full of idle boats unable to fish for fear of breaking government quotas, their owners forced to stay home broke, bankers screaming for cash. A row of shop fronts, festooned with strings of coloured bulbs, shone in the late afternoon light and a chemist lay a hundred yards to their right. "Ok, stockings," she said.

They entered through swing doors and a convector heater, high above their heads, exhaled a jet of hot humid air about their persons, blowing their hair about their faces, warming the backs of their necks. She scanned the displays in the hope of finding what she was looking for without too much trouble and on discovering the goods in question changed there right in the middle of the aisle. (There was no one about and the only checkout girl was filing her nails in deep apathetic dontcare.)

They purchased a packet of sugar-free gum then left.

**

From there they made for an eatery tutored in the art of make believe where burger and burger bun were offered on transfer covered plate and taken in reciprocal acknowledgement that all was not what it seemed. Ellis could hardly believe his eyes and as they seated themselves in the corner a fat girl with a bucket and mop who'd appeared from inside the gent's toilet handed them paper hats. He lifted the burger and bit it in half with gnashing teeth like a rabid dog on a feeding frenzy then pushed the other half, the one that was left, in the direction of Joyce: "See, no salad!" They both laughed hysterically. "Oh well," he said.

"Goes with the seats I suppose; fuckin ladybirds."

It was now completely dark on the outside and the area directly below the promenade was illuminated by lights from the street and by the great flashing arc from the lighthouse at the mouth of the harbour. They went down to the sand and as he bent to pick a smooth flat stone, she grabbed him from behind, cupping his scrotum in the palm of her hand. He came up smiling and let go the smooth obsidian like piece of rock he'd gathered, sending it out across the flat expanse of sea: One ... two, it died ... Again ... One ... two, it died ... She ... Plop, it died ... He ... One, it died ... He she ... One, one, two, they died ... two ... three ... four ... They played for twenty minutes, until finally they were beat by the cold and returned to the car for the long journey home where the sham of unfamiliarity once again assumed control, everything back to the accustomed ritual of nodding their hellos in passing and two or three minutes small talk whilst ordering at the bar.

**

"Pint of Guinness Joyce ... Enjoy your day off yesterday?"

She removed a measure from under the counter and began to pull the thick black stout, watching as it billowed up the side of the glass, filled; then slowly began to settle. "Quite nice, thanks," she answered, without so much as a smile. "Yourself?"

He told her he'd gone to the coast for the day and had been forced to return early due to the weather. Rather disappointing. He paid for the drink then looked for a seat.

Over in a corner the boys were playing poker and he decided to try his luck. Billy dealt him in, and he exchanged two cards immediately, lifting them to complete a royal flush and take the pot.

"Where the hell did you get to yesterday?" Simon asked him, lifting his eyes from behind the paper he was reading to draw him a look of bewildered puzzlement. "We looked everywhere for you." Ellis lifted an ace king five, two still on the table and smiled: "Some days I like to be by myself," he answered.

"Others I like to disappear altogether."

*

BOOK ONE

*

A silverskin onion, cheddar cheese and pineapple skewered on a stick.

1

The funny thing is, is that marriage had always been the last thing on our minds, and those who knew us wouldn't have put us down as an item, and if they had, would certainly not have put the relationship down as having legs and lasting as long as it did. The defining factor in that show, in the end - the one that did finish us off and the one that none of us foresaw or may have seen - a fucked-up bat disease that managed to escape from the less than secure Wuhan Institute of Virology in China. Or to give it its official title, SARS-CoV-2.

Anyway, be that as it may, Joyce was gone along with the twenty-four thousand-odd other poor souls that were left to die on their own; thrown in the back of a refrigerated truck, awaiting her slot to be cremated. Stuffed in an oven with no one there to give her a final farewell. Her ashes now kept in a glazed jardiniere, that sits on a stand at the foot of the hall, where I burn my daily offering of incense. Nag Champa my scent of choice. That or Flora Fluxo. A stick at a time their ash mixing in as they burn on down to the wood.

And the funny thing was, it wasn't so very perceptible at first, yet I was sure she was putting on weight.

She'd have loved that one. That's where her sense of humour lay. Along those lines. Out on the periphery. It wasn't in the norm. Things that others considered discriminatory would set her off on a fit. Black jokes, fat jokes, ethnic jokes and farting. She didn't grasp political correctness. I think it was anathema to her. She was unable to get her head round it, and no matter how I tried to explain it to her she always ended up with a blank expression on her face as if, "What the fuck is he talking about?"

I tried.

And on more than one occasion she told me to shut the fuck up and leave her alone. She didn't mean anything by it she'd say, it was the way she was built. It was so much simpler in the seventies, she'd go on. No one bothered their arse. A racist was the last thing she was, she said. "I think it's to do with my age.

What was wrong with Bernard Manning anyway?" she'd say. "Eh? Tell me that? Nothing. Him and Roy Chubby Brown. Freddie Starr and Jim Davidson. You got a laugh with those guys. Not like the lot we have now. So don't tell me about political correctness, woke or cancel culture. Nonsense, that's all it is. Sexism and LGBT rights? What the fuck is that all about? I don't get it."

And she didn't.

A new age creature she was not.

I lost count of the number of times I had to silence her and get her to drop the tone of her voice a notch in the supermarket or bank. Or in a restaurant in the city where we'd gone to enjoy the fare. Indian or Argentinian usually, now and again Chinese. And that one put the fear of death in me. I don't know what it was about a Chinese establishment, she always lost it completely when we chose that particular country's cuisine as the go to of an evening. The Great Wall or Mrs Chan's. She'd lose control of her tongue, and it would take on a life of its own.

She'd put on a Chinese accent and run with it. Then the second I'd pull her up on it - letting her know in no uncertain terms it was downright rude and she was out of order, she'd inform me it made it easier for them to understand what she was saying and carry on as before. She was a nightmare. Yet having said that, I loved her despite her faults and the fact she was stuck in the seventies and eighties - firmly wedged to the point that no amount of wiggle was likely to remove her - my feelings for her didn't change.

We *were* an item and that was that, and we didn't care what anyone was thinking. To hell with them. If they didn't like it, go fuck. I knew she was bloody rock-and-rolling; that was part of her charm. That's what attracted me to her - that and her laissez-faire.

"Devil-may-care," she used to say. "And that's the way I like it.

We'll be dead soon enough, and you know that. So, we might as well enjoy ourselves, as long as we have our health."

She'd do random things out of the blue, like a week in a cave in Spain. I mean. Who the hell goes to Spain for a week then spends it living in a cave? And I asked her this. "A hobbit?" It didn't make any sense at the time and still doesn't. Off we'd go.

Bags packed and airport here we come. Sacromonte to a hole in the wall like Wilma and Fred, constantly on edge with the worry that any minute Dino'd come charging through the door and flatten us both. Laid out cold on the cold stone floor.

Nevertheless, it was free, and trying to imagine a better week was almost impossible, although it did have a downside: You had to take a week to recover on return to feel half normal again. Recharge your depleted batteries, and shower to remove the grime. Despite this the people were nice and made us welcome without a hint of delving into our business. And I liked that. Keeping our noses out of others business was the thing we prided ourselves on. If it didn't directly affect us, then we didn't want to know. It was up to others how they saw fit to run their lives and so long as it wasn't impinging on ours or anyone else's then carry on. "If you mind your own business," as old Hank used to say, "then you won't be minding mine." And as a rule of thumb, that about summed us up. More than happy to go with the flow and take things as they came. Singing as we slaved was not for us. We were free to do as we liked. We answered to no one and didn't break the rules. Well, not so much as you'd notice. A bit of dope now and again. Booze was our bag, and so long as it was flowing on tap, so to speak, we were happy as pigs in shit. Booze and travel to interesting places, that's what did it for us.

A week or two at the Faslane Peace Camp another of her zany do's.

I always went along for the hell of things, and always enjoyed the ride. I didn't engage in politics in any meaningful level. It was more a thing to moan about than anything. Joyce was a different fish.

She'd made the acquaintance of a member of the CND when visiting an aunt in Oban in 1985, and had grown quite close, becoming a ban-the-bomber herself, albeit not a fully paid-up, card-carrying, member. More of a weekend sort of player, willing to go on the odd march here and there; not so fanatical as to join the hardcore on their fulltime camp-out, in the cold and pissing rain. Argyll and Bute, a wild and desolate place on the best of days, not only the depths of winter. Whereas Evie was made of different stuff and as far as I recall stayed with the camp several years before moving on to pastures new. The last we heard she was campaigning in the south for the Green Party, an aging hippy, her hair still in trademark dreads.

The camp itself was fun, if you managed to remove the politics and banner-waving side of things and focus on the camaraderie, striking up friendships as you moved from caravan to caravan. And much akin the Spanish caves, a good shower and feet-up on our return was needed to reacclimatize. I'm positive - thinking back on it now - from Joyce's point of view, that like the caves in Spain, if the option had been available to her, we'd have taken up residency full-time in either one. Still, necessity called; because at that time, we were both in full employment, working for the man, living a life of domesticity, or near as dammit. However, others looking in were likely to have drawn their own conclusion: "Work shy bastards," as we did spend a large amount of time between jobs. To hell with what others thought they thought. Who were the bloody mugs? Not us, working a lifetime for a pittance. What would be the point of that? It didn't make sense. It only served to tie you down. Three or four month out each year afforded you a modicum of freedom. A freedom to travel wherever you liked, within your budget of course. A freebie here and there, always repaid in kind. People we'd met would come and stay. It was different then. Work was easy come easy go. Leave a job Friday and by Monday be employed again. It wasn't as it is now. Jobs were ten a penny.

That was the lifestyle we led, and it suited us fine.

Work double shifts till we saved a bit. Travel then dive back in.

Money spent, then save again. Straight back into the grind.

2

We reconnected - neither of us having laid eyes on the other for a number of years - in the winter of 75/76.

It had been the mildest winter in almost a hundred years, and as a result I was looking forward to summer, hoping to hell we were going to have a good one as I no doubt believed we would if the winter was anything to go by. And we did. It exceeded expectations, and by the end of it I was more swarthy than usual. My over-all colour a deep, dark brown. My flip flops fit for the bin.

I digress.

The Who had charted with a number called Squeeze Box, and things looked to be on the up. I'd gained employment at The Biscuit Factory after three and a half month on the dole and was pleased to be part of the human race again - having reason, at last, to climb from bed and contribute to society. Integrate on whatever level.

Maybe not employment on a glamourous level in some respects; employment none the less. Nothing that taxed the old grey matter. Clock yourself in and out. Do your time, eight till five. Home by six, then fed. A Vesta curry or Spam fritters, topped with a crispy fried egg. Then round it off with a bowl of jelly, covered in evaporated milk. Settle down in front of the box and watch whatever was on. The

Sweeny or a similar programme. My head was normally in a book by that time of night. The tv more for background noise than for anything I'd watch. Then as soon as the music for Roobarb kicked-in, the book was snapped to the shut. Dropped to the floor by the chair where I sat, or side of the couch where I lay. Nothing distracted when Roobarb was on, my attention gripped in a vice. The voice of Richard Briers did it, along with the shaky cartoon. Each tiny episode - five minutes long - etched in my brain for life. That pink mouse and the Sun and Moon. Roobarb eating coal and chairs. Roobarb eating anything he got his hands on. Custard the cunning saboteur. Five nights a week, before the news, everything came to a halt. Things stood still for those five minutes, then proceeded as before. Supper at nine - toasted cheese - bed by half past twelve. Read for another hour. Lights out, up for work.

And the first Monday there - at The Biscuit Factory - delighted beyond belief.

I'd been set to work, after the initial induction in an office on the third floor, on the Jammie Dodger line, and after an hour of standing watching others pack, I was more than glad to hear the horn that signalled the announcement for a break. "Not before time," I said out loud. "Now where the hell's the canteen?"

I followed the others along with my nose, till I reached the end of a queue.

The choice was simple. Two on black pudding ... One on sausage and egg.

I sat with a woman called Maggie and her friends. Then after we'd finished the food we'd been eating we drank tea and smoked cigarettes. The conversation then turned to the prowess of their men in the sack of a night.

My god, I couldn't believe my ears. I hadn't heard the likes of this in I don't know how long, and it took all my powers of the here and now to remind myself it was middle aged women I was with who stuffed biscuits into trays in a biscuit factory in the city for a living, rather than grown men sitting at a table in an engineering plant - page three pictures tacked to the walls - covered in oil and swarf. They were funny however. And when Maggie started to relate how her husband was on longer than a dumpling, as she put it, when they were at it, I felt I was about to burst. Shit, tea, and Jammie Dodger sprayed across the table, as Carol said, "Sounds like my man. He can't hold back either. "Doesn't have an ounce of control."

"Mine's the same," quipped Agnes, in response. "All mouth and trousers. Likes to think he's god's gift. Unfortunately, it's always a sprint. Never a marathon, I can tell you. Always goes off half-cocked."

"Ha … Half-cocked," said Vera, as she drew on her cig. "Mine's the same. Full of great ideas at the time, then done before he starts. Two minutes later he's lying there like a bat in a state of torpor. Doesn't move a muscle the rest of the night. Might as well be dead for all the use he is. Hope we don't get burgled."

"Buggered?" said Lynn, in a tone of surprise. "I should be so lucky."

Then I heard a voice at my back. I knew who it was right away.

"Jeffery Ellis, is that you? Tell me that's not you?"

I turned and our eyes locked. I knew it was her right away.

"Joyce Arnold," I said with a smile. "Long time no see. How are you?"

She pulled up a chair then squeezed herself in at the corner of the table by Maggie.

"Not bad," she said. "Much better for seeing you."

She tapped a cigarette from Agnus, then lit the thing from a match. Blew it out then dropped it to the floor, kicked it under the table.

"So, what brings you here?" she asked, as if it wasn't obvious.

"Work. Started this morning. Jammie Dodger line."

She laughed as if it were a joke. "The Jammie Dodger line?"

"Yes. The Jammie Dodger Line. I think you've got to start there."

We both burst into laughter.

The Jammie Dodger line.

She was on Wagon Wheels, soon to be demoted to Viscount.

We laughed … Our sense of humour was stranger than most.

By the end of the break, we'd arranged to meet at the gate at the end of the shift.

Six hours after our unexpected meeting we were sitting at the bar in a pub in the city.

It was nice to see her again. Unexpected, in the canteen of The Biscuit Factory. That would have been the last place I'd have come up with if asked where I might bump into her if we were likely to meet again. Yet, I suspect coming up with any location where you were likely to bump into Joyce was damn near impossible the way she moved around. Staying put for any longer than three or four month in one place was not part of her modus operandi. She liked to shift house and job and didn't put down roots.

She looked well.

And to see her now, minus the hairnet and protective overcoat she'd been wearing earlier in the day, was better. Her hair was shorter than I remembered it being - cropped - though not so short it prevented her wearing a snap clip. The stockings she'd once wore with such in-your-face, youthful effervescence had also gone, and she'd now taken to wearing thick black leggings under a black zip front cord mini skirt - slightly longer than days gone by - and black Dr. Martins boots. This was topped with a Black Sabbath tee shirt and a black knit hooded cardi.

We ordered drinks then settled, our knees making contact as we faced each other on the high wooden stools where we sat.

"Cheers.

So," I said, "are you still in touch with any of the old gang … you know, Billy or Simon or any of those guys? I've not seen them since I left."

"I didn't keep in touch. Lost contact. You know how it is. People disappear from the radar, and friendships you once considered important turn out to be nothing more than what they were; friendships. I lost touch over time. I can't say what they're up to these days or if they're still in touch with one another.

Probably still sitting in the same seats they occupied in that bar I used to work. They always were creatures of habit and didn't venture far, as you know. They'll still be there when they're skeletons," she said. "Smoking and drinking beer."

A vision of them all as bone-men flashed and it wasn't a pretty sight.

"Can you imagine," I said, "the lot of them sitting there rattling away, beer on the floor and seats? The entire bar awash with lager as the stuff pours straight out through them."

Mop-man in with a bucket and mop trying to keep it down. Tables and chairs floating off to the distance, the jukebox throwing off sparks. Cutlasses drawn; the barman forced to walk the plank, over the edge to his death. "Varmint … Cleeve him to the brisket boys, then batten down the hatches."

"I don't know how they managed it," she said. "Especially on the dole. They always had money for cigarettes and beer. Horses and dominos as well. I don't know how they did it. If you ask me, it's a mystery. I can't figure it out. People come and go."

She had a point. Most people do come and go, and most people you associate with are nothing more than that, associates. A few, if any at all, turn out to be friends in the true sense of the word. When the chips are down and you need them, that's when they show their true colours, and nine out of ten it's black.

I told her I'd lost contact myself. And didn't know where they were.

"Might as well as dropped off the planet, for all I know where they are."

We finished our drinks then made for the street, deciding it was time we were home.

We said we'd see each other tomorrow, at breakfast in the canteen.

Joyce lived a ten-minute walk away. My own was more like fifteen.

3

We began to meet regularly after this, both at work then later when things developed.

I suppose it was inevitable, looking back on it, our relationship blossomed and took the direction it did after that initial meeting and catch-up on my first day at The Biscuit Factory. All the same, no one could possibly have seen it coming, even with a crystal ball.

If you'd asked us, two or three year ago, if there was any possibility of getting together, I think we'd have laughed and walked away.

That's how unlikely that was ever about to take off.

It wasn't on the cards and that was that, and nobody saw it coming.

Stranger things have happened.

People abducted by aliens then returned to their cars or beds.

Poltergeist that terrorize families and voices from the other side.

So, in all probability the odds of Joyce and myself hooking up the way we did were not as slim as we imagined, and the odds a little on the shorter side than anyone anticipated.

Stranger things have happened as I said, like to sailors when far away at sea.

Then after several weeks together it was time to go public. The people we worked with in The Biscuit Factory had suspected as much, saying they already knew when we told them.

"You'd have to have been in blinkers," they said, "or have your head buried in sand not to have seen that coming. You were all over each other in the canteen. We were going to tell you to get a room, things were getting that hot. We didn't know where to look. Congratulations anyway. Try to control yourselves."

We weren't cognizant we were acting in such a manner. We were in love.

LOVE.

And whatever else it did for us, it made us laugh. It made us laugh, looking back at the time we'd spent together in the past, to think we were now in love. The way we behaved in those days couldn't be looked on as romantic. More animalistic than anything. And the number of partners we'd managed to get through we'd lost count of long ago. Anyway, who was counting? And who cared? We weren't about to kill; not for a gossipy tongue. Let them get on with their tawdry lives. We were living the dream. Living in the now, getting on with things. Not the type to look back.

Forward march and don't spare the hearses. No use living in the past. We were living in the here and now. The only thing you can do.

By the end of March, I had given up my flat and moved in with Joyce full-time.

It made sense, as I was already spending three to four days a week there as it was, and paying rent on two apartments was nonsensical from an economical standpoint. It let us save for any up-and-coming travel we planned, and the amount of time we'd be able to spend together outweighed everything else. When we sized it up it became a no-brainer. Then three days later I was in. Two case of clothing, a bag of books, a dozen LPs. I walked out and left the lot, apart from the things I'd need.

I put my toothpaste and brush in the bathroom along with my aftershave.

"Do you fancy eating out tonight?" she said.

"I think that's a good idea. Anywhere particular in mind?"

"How about the Rendezvous on Queensferry Street. It's a bit on the pricey side; what the hell. We've been paid. And it is our first night living together as a couple. Might as well start as we mean to go on. And we'll take a taxi. Deal?"

"Deal," I said, with a smile on my face. "Do you happen to have any paint? Maureen in the work is looking for paint. Said any colour will do."

"Maureen?" she asked, surprised. "Why does she want paint?"

"I didn't ask. Said she needed paint."

I dumped the rest of my stuff in the bedroom awaiting my allocated drawers.

"There are tins in the cupboard in the hall. Two or three. I don't know there's any gloss. Was it gloss she said she was looking for?"

"Don't know. Said she needed paint. That's as much as I know. I'll take whatever's there, then leave it at that. If she doesn't like it, she can go to the hardware store. She only asked for paint."

Joyce went out to buy a loaf, returned with bacon and eggs.

I dropped a copy of Transformer onto the music-centre in the living room then turned the volume to high.

Joyce was frying up in the kitchen, the aroma smelling good.

Sizzle.

"Ready." she shouted, her head round the door. "Tea or coffee or juice?"

God.

My belly was ready for a feast. I hadn't eaten since dinner last night, what with getting ready for the move.

I sat down opposite Joyce, at the table, then started to butter toast. I poured myself a mug of tea. Joyce was on the juice.

Eggs, bacon, potato scone. Mushroom, black pudding, and beans. Sausage with lashings of HP sauce. Cerebos salt from a can.

"You know," said Joyce. "I always meant to ask … The day we went to the seaside … Did you tell anyone about it?"

I remembered the experience well and intended not to forget.

I shoved in a mouthful of sausage then chewed, then looked her straight in the eye.

"Only Johnny," I said, when I'd swallowed. No one else."

She rested her knife and fork on her plate then spoke with awe and wonder.

"You know Johnny?" she asked, with excitement, as if he were Santa Claus. "You literally know

Johnny? The guy who writes those crazy stories then posts them through your door? Nobody knows Johnny," she said. "How do you know Johnny?"

"I just know him. That's all. I just know him."

"How?" she continued, like a dog with a bone. She wasn't for letting go.

My breakfast was getting cold. I took a slice of crispy bacon then folded it into toast.

"I don't know. I've known him all my life. Primary school, I think. Not sure. When the stories started to come in my curiosity piqued.

It was seventy-two. We received a copy of *Number fifty-nine, in camera*, and it rang a bell. It was the ending that struck me as familiar when I read it. The familiarity struck a chord.

All that talk of the peaks of Haushan in Shaanxi and the hermits that lived there. I put two and two together and come up with Grantham MacGregor, a kid I'd went to school with. I still wasn't a hundred per cent positive it was him. I needed something more substantial to run with. The thing was - at the time - he kept going on about zen masters and hermits that made their homes there and spoke constantly on the subject. So, when I met him in a bar a year later, I spun him a yarn. You know - as we were still getting these things through our door - make a positive ID."

I cleaned my plate with a slice of bread then poured myself more tea.

"I fed him a line or two. I told him of the time we'd gone to the coast and spent the day by ourselves.

Six weeks later *The b job, sugar-free death machine,* made an appearance and I had my proof."

"And all that talk of the sex and stuff, where the hell did he get that? That's not what happened, and you know it. He didn't change our names."

"Poetical licence as far as I know. You know what these writers are like. You tell them so-and-so's been feeling ill and before you know it, they're dead. Died of a mysterious illness only contractable through sex. They have this inordinate need to beef things up out of all proportion and before you know what you've got, a snowball has rolled to a thundering mass hurtling headlong downhill. No probability of stopping the thing, completely out of control.

Michael's in hospital. He's hurt his hand.

Michael got shot in the gut.

That's the type of thing they come up with. And they get away with whatever."

"What did you say his name was again?"

"His name was Grantham MacGregor."

"I don't know him," she said. "I know of Johnny … Everyone knows of Johnny … They don't know who he is … They only know the name."

*"… Oh, no one calls me on the telephone
I put another record on my stereo
but I'm still singing a song of you
it's a lonely Saturday night …"*

"I don't know him that well myself," I said. "It was only at school. Once we left, and went our separate ways, the contact was lost. It was only when that first story came through the door, and I put two and two together he sprang to mind. Then when I fed him that stuff where we went to the coast and the *sugar-free* came in, that clinched it. Two and two make five, and there you have it. Bingo. Grantham MacGregor.

Still, haven't seen him in a long time. Don't know where he lives."

We tidied up then washed the dishes. Went for the weekly shop.

Well, when I say weekly, the way we ate it ended up lasting four days and then we had to replenish. Most of it tinned stuff. Fresh meat products we kept in the fridge. Frozen stuff was mostly out of the question as the small freezer it contained was barely large enough to house a packet of frozen fish fingers along with a half dozen burgers. We managed. That was the way things were in those days and we didn't question them. It was more than likely a 1960s second-hand job to begin with, or third-hand for all we knew. It was good enough and did the job. Held milk and eggs as well. Tomatoes, cucumber, and lettuce. Four thin slices of corned beef, wrapped in grease proof paper. Cans of lager and a bottle of juice, the thing was damn near full. A quarter of spam would have tipped it over, stuffed to the gunwales and more. A constant buzz that drove us insane, we were waiting for the thing to explode.

How it kept things fresh was a mystery to us.

We finished the unpacking then went to bed. Slept till half-past five.

We were dressed and ready for the off by seven.

Seated in the Rendezvous by nine.

We'd had a number of drinks before gaining the place and already were feeling quite good. We ordered a bottle of Liebfraumilch and studied the menu till it came.

That's when they started. The racist remarks. Although we didn't realise it at the time.

It was off the cuff stuff; none the less racist. Social stereotypes formed over years that were outside our conscious awareness. Views that conflicted with our own conscious values and we didn't know.

What did they expect to come out of our mouths with what they were feeding us from the box?

Love Thy Neighbour, Till Death Do Us Part, The Black and White Minstrel Show. And that was only starters. The list was as long as your arm. Day after day, pounding away, relentless insidious bile. Drip-fed constantly year by year, decade after decade.

Flied lice. Lubely chicken. Chinkie and take a wok.

And it wasn't solely confined to Southeast Asian establishments either. Indian and Bangladeshi establishments were fair game as well. Especially when they emptied out the pubs and the drunks poured in through their doors. The abuse meted out in those establishments vile and pernicious at best.

Abusive racists who when sobered up you'd never label as such.

Mind Your Language. It Ain't Half Hot Mum. Spike, in Curry & Chips.

We ordered chow mein, chips with gravy. A bowl of fried rice on the side.

Home by midnight we went to bed where we smoked a cigarette between us.

"You see," said Joyce when she'd taken a puff. "That's the trouble with eating Chinese food … half an hour later you're hungry again."

Monday came round before we knew it and the biscuits were calling again.

I lifted a tin of paint for Maureen and deemed it drunk. A sticker on its lid made me laugh when I saw it, printed in large black bold:

Keep me
upright
and secure
on your
way home.

It doesn't get better than that.

It seemed to.

Summer eventually arrived.

4

As I suspected, at the time, the mild winter was indeed a prelude to an unbelievable summer.

It was so sticky people were lying wherever they fell, stripped to their underwear - blue, black, grey, red, and washed-out white.

Each inch of available space had been taken over by bodies. Requisitioned for sunning themselves in a bid of attaining a tan.

It was the best year of our lives and being young only added to the sense of excitement, as a drought set in, and we were forced to collect water from standpipes in the street.

It was a summer to behold, and the one all summers from here on in was measured against.

We supposed it mightn't end, and on weekends we'd take to the Gardens as early as possible in the hope of getting a spot. Then once there we'd lie all day, till the sun went down, then home. Always by foot to mingle with the throng of people on the city streets.

It was as if every nationality was there sitting on the grass, bookended by the castle and the monument erected to Scott, eating ice cream and cake.

They baked.

Factor thirty was out of the question as was factor fifty.

Anti-bake lotion was anathema to most, especially the locals. And if you'd broached the subject that skin cancer was the likely outcome for failure to take care of this organ you'd probably have been looked on with credulity. "Whit? Whit the fuck are you oan aboot? Who said anything aboot cancer?"

The sun baked down, and they slowly turned red like lobsters fresh from the pot.

We loved it, and Saturdays and Sundays we were there - as long as the heatwave lasted - and always packed a picnic. Enough to last the entire day, well on into the night.

We always tried our best to be there by seven or eight in the morning to get the pick of the spots before the crowds poured in; and we normally inclined toward the Waverley end. Once there we'd spread our travel rug - an old, bobbly, Mackintosh tartan thing Joyce had bought second-hand - then once satisfied with our position in the great scheme of things, that was us for the day, or till the call of nature grabbed us and we were forced to either use the conveniences at the West End of the Gardens or cross the road to Waverley Station and make use of the facilities on offer there, although more than not the choice had been made for us and we opted for the West End pissoir, that being free of charge. Only the station's John when things really caught us short, and time was of the essence. Then we'd be running up those stairs, across the road, down the ramp and in. Back in ten with fresh cans of juice purchased in the concourse shop. Only. Only if seriously caught and feeling flush at the time. The exorbitant prices charged in the station to piss and buy juice enough to put anyone in their right mind off, so usually we used the West End.

A quick piss there than a slow walk back, taking in the sights as we went. People-watching as we strolled along, making our way back to base.

And it was base.

A thousand bases.

People had set up camp where they could. On any old piece of land.

Base camp on Everest sprang to mind, minus two or three lines of Lung ta and snow that was over our feet. It looked for all its worth as if an assault on the Scott Monument - that great Victorian gothic carbuncle that sat up level with the street - were about to take place, last one to the top a shitter.

Radios blared a selection of tunes from Jolene to I Love to Boogie. Our particular transistor set: Back In The USSR.

Our rug was laid and ready for the day. We lay there side by side.

Cakes, and corned beef sandwiches with tomato, smothered in Heinz Salad Cream. A bottle of Barr's American Cream Soda. Two Mar's bars, Two Aztec bars. Two packets of Tooty Frooties. A half dozen packets of assorted crisps and four large bottles of cider. And in case we felt a sudden urge, two jars of pickled mussels; which we'd eat with a toothpick straight from the jar then down the juice in one. Lie back down on our messy rug and let the rays do their best.

It was like a burns unit after the first two weeks. Blondes and redheads that should have known better than to lie out in these conditions fried to a crisp. And you'd have been forgiven for thinking you'd been transported to a WWI field hospital, especially with the one o'clock gun. *BANG!*

Still, they lay there cooking away, determined to crisp or die.

The country sweltered with a smile on its face then abruptly it came to an end.

It rained from September well into October. Dismay at the arrival of floods.

"Who'd have thunk it a month ago?" said Joyce, as we stood in the kitchen." And I took it, from the manner in which she spoke, it was directed at no one in particular.

She was staring through the window at the rain outside, dancing on the tarmac below.

"It doesn't seem possible," she said, "when you think about it. All that sunshine then suddenly this. Who the hell would have thunk it? Soon be dark from three in the afternoon till nine o'clock in the morning."

I was convinced she was rambling, so left it at that. Let her get on with things.

Her sister had arrived that afternoon with news concerning their gran.

She'd been ill for months, the rapid onset of frailty over the preceding weeks causing the family concern. Then after a meeting of various members of the family they'd drawn the conclusion the best place to put her, for everyone's piece of mind, was the local nursing home; and arrangements were now being made.

Joyce already knew all this of course and decided to play it dumb.

"So, whose idea was it to put her in a care home?"

"The family's," said Janine. "It was a joint decision."

"Wasn't much of a joint decision if I was excluded," said Joyce.

She turned and looked her sister in the eye. A look that screamed out, Bitch. "Now, was it?"

I took myself to the shop for cigs. This was way beyond me. In my experience the two of them were best left to their own devices when dealing with stuff that concerned their gran. Family business was family business and nothing to do with me. Besides, Joyce was well versed when it came to the affairs of her grandmother and was already quite aware of the plans to put her in a home. They'd been in constant communication since Joyce left home at the age of fifteen to travel, what with weekly phone calls and postcards. She knew of their plans to offload her in a home. Gran had told her months ago and told her to keep it to herself. She was.

I grabbed my coat then left in silence. Neither of them saw me go.

"We didn't want to worry you, that's all," her sister said.

"Worry me, is that it? More like, let's leave Joyce out of it altogether. Is it not?"

"I don't know why I bother," said Janine. "It's always the same with you. You're always hard done by. It's always poor Joyce. She's barely functioning as it is, Joyce. A decision had to be made. So, it was. It was either that or we were going to walk in one day and find her dead on the floor. She's not safe on her own anymore. Does that not make sense?"

"Of course it makes sense," said Joyce. "It's the not being included I find the problem."

"Well, what do you expect when we don't see you from one years end to another. We're not aware of where you live half the time. Finding you isn't that easy you know. I had to contact one of your old neighbours to find out if she had any idea where you'd gone. No one knew your whereabouts. It took a bit of doing to find you."

"I don't think it was as difficult as you make out. That's your problem Janine. Everything's a chore. You were the same as a child. Everything was a chore then and nothing's changed. Always another's fault. If you'd have asked gran, she'd have been able to tell you where I was. She knew where I was living. She always knows where I am."

"You don't listen, do you?" said Janine. "That's one of the reasons she's not able to live on her own anymore; she can't recall things. You won't listen, will you? Self-centred, that's your problem, Joyce. Bloody well self-centred."

I bought the cigs then considered a coffee. Fifteen minutes was not enough for the two of them to sort this out.

"Self-centred my ass," said Joyce. "You lot think you're the Masons. Everything's a secret. You're full of shite Janine and you know it. Full of fucking shite."

"That's right," her sister said. "Stoop to the depths of the gutter. Look at you. Working at a dead-end job in a biscuit factory and living with a useless get. You'll never amount to anything.

"Suits me fine," said Joyce, with a smile. "Bloody well suits me fine. Who'd want to end up living like you, up to your eyes in debt? Fur coat and no knickers that's you. Driving about in your big fancy car, living on spam and chips. Posh house in a posh estate and up to your eyes in debt."

"Huh. Better than the pigsty you live in. Look at the place. Looks like it hasn't been cleaned in weeks, and I've no doubt it hasn't. The place is a shithole Joyce, and you know it. And anyway, the decision's been made. She goes to a home a week come Tuesday, whether you like it or not. Mum and I have made the decision along with uncle Ron. That's all I came to tell you Joyce, so now I'll be saying goodbye."

She lifted her jacket and bag from the chair then quietly walked out the door."

"Good riddance," said Joyce, under her breath, as she closed the door at her back. She filled the kettle. "Bitch."

I was back about ten minutes later and glad to find Joyce on her own.

I was happy to find her sister gone, for the simple reason the two of them arguing in close proximity to me made me feel uneasy. I was better out of it. That way they got on with it without the distraction of me sitting listening. Especially as Janine considered it none of my business. Plus, I was a Catholic to boot. And anyway, Joyce always related everything that happened on my return, so my being there to see things as they unfolded - live - wasn't necessary.

Out of sight, out of mind, and I liked to keep it like that.

I poured the tea that was left in the pot then sat down to talk with Joyce.

We knew the score and had done for a while. Janine turning up the way she had was a waste of time. Though Joyce being Joyce would never have told her as much and was more than happy to have her travel from her home in the borders then make the return journey fuming, as no doubt she would.

They weren't close to begin with, and what had been happening to her gran over the past six month only served to widen the gulf and drive the wedge that already existed between them further home. She could have intervened, and re-enforced her wish her gran stayed put, even if she'd given her assurance it wouldn't happen and was sticking to her word.

We'd discussed the inevitability of her being institutionalised then realised we couldn't prevent it.

Her frailty was becoming an issue, and her immobility was dramatically contributing to an increased rate of muscle loss, which over the three or four month leading up to Christmas was a lot more pronounced than ever.

Her memory was fading, and this gave rise to the possibility it may be dementia. However, Joyce had explained they were talking crap and had passed this on to gran.

"They're only trying to ship you off and get their hands on your things. That's all they're up to gran, believe me. And if I have any say that's the last thing they'll do."

Nevertheless, she was frail, and living more in social isolation than ever; the others only turning up when they suspected there was something to be gained. And once her bathing became a problem, that was once a week. Descending on her bathroom like vultures overhead, circling, awaiting her death. Ready to swoop and pick at her bones till stripped of their last piece of flesh.

They were in for a shock. Uninstructed an ignorant bliss.

Gran would laugh the last.

Because the week after Joyce turned eighteen, gran in her great wisdom, and not wishing the others to get their grubby hands on whatever she left when she'd gone, amended her will and left the lot to her favourite grandchild Joyce.

Her only regret, she'd told Joyce, was she wouldn't be there to see their faces. She'd die in the knowledge they wouldn't be happy, and that was good enough.

By the end of the year we had moved from the city and were living west of the Calders.

Gran had died in the summer of seventy-seven and the distribution of her will had been made in December. Joyce had taken possession of her property by the middle of the month, and we were in by Christmas.

It was one less burden to deal with, and we were glad of it. We'd both moved jobs and were now working at E.P.S. (Moulders) LTD, Livingston, in the manufacture of engineered foam products along with polystyrene packaging and handling solutions for the pharmaceutical industry.

Joyce was employed in the store side of things, I was in seating components.

Now with no mortgage or rent eating away at our cash, things were looking up.

And they were.

The move to gran's opened up a whole new episode for us, as for the first time we were able to save each month. It was like we'd won The Pools, and the rest of the family were jealous. Seething. Foaming at the mouth like rabid dogs after Joyce had been left the lot. House. Car in the drive. Jewellery, and things. And all her money to boot. Which, after everything had been finalised, amounted to a tidy sum.

Two and a half thousand pound, to be exact, seventy-five new pence.

Christmas dinner our first year in was the best we'd had. And at Joyce's insistence we started off with a decadent ring of prawns. What the hell was happening here, a decadent ring of prawns? Shit, who the hell would have thunk it; a decadent ring of prawns? We were climbing the ladder and no mistake.

I didn't know such things existed, then to see one there in the middle of the table almost blew my mind.

We next moved on to turkey and sprouts, stuffing, and cranberry sauce. We were living it up, high off the hog, and had trouble cramming it in.

Gravy and carrots, roast potatoes, pigs in blankets and peas.

We omitted the parsnips, neither of us keen. Then Christmas pudding with cream.

Twenty minutes later we were lying on the couch, utterly fit to burst. Gran looking on from her urn on the mantel, no doubt with a smile on her face. Holly, ivy, and mistletoe adorning her sky-blue urn.

We'd knocked it off and knew it. We were grateful for what she'd done. Janine and the rest of the family raging, they saw it in a different light. And the word that reached us by the end of May, was they'd said they were going to contest. They didn't. They were merely sore losers and that was that. They'd rampage their passion for as long as it took then finally get on with their lives. Stewing in their juices until finally tender, well and truly done.

By six o'clock we were ready for seconds. Joyce put together a plate.

5

The house was off the road about a quarter mile and sat in an acre of land. And surrounded by trees the way it was afforded perfect seclusion if that's what you required. You had to know it was there to begin with or else you'd be quite unaware.

Gran had loved it and was more than happy, in her later years, to live the life of a semi-recluse; four or five month were she lived by herself, and then it was open house. Usually in the summer when the sun was up, and the table could be set outdoors - under the pergola draped in Clematis - heavy with charcuterie and wine.

It was heaven to Joyce, and she remembered it with great affection from the times she'd spent there as a child with her grandmother and grandfather in the years leading up to his death in the summer of 69. A place of childhood dreams and memories she hoped to have till the end.

"See. Here," she said, "take a look at this." Then led me out by the arm.

Everything was coated in a heavy hoar frost, thick as leaves on a tree.

We walked to the table then she brushed it off with the sleeve of her duffle coat.

"See."

A beautiful OM Mandala in black, gold, red, and blue had been painted in the middle of the thing.

"Oils," she said.

"I was spending the summer of 67 here when we painted that. Well, when I say we, what I really mean is Walter, my grandfather. I always called him by his first name at his own insistence. Said he wasn't the grandfather type so best stick to Walter. And I did.

He gave it a coat of light clear varnish when it dried, to finish it off.

We carved our names on three of its edges then month and year on the fourth."

WALTER, HATTIE, JOYCE. JULY 10TH - 26TH 1967.

"We were proud when we finished it and rightly so. Still looks good today. Two month later he was diagnosed with cancer. Two years later he was dead.

That's when I moved in full-time with gran and lived until I left school. Myself, gran and her chickens. She always said the place would be mine as soon as she popped her clogs. And true to her word, as soon as she started to go into decline, she finally signed it over, with the proviso I took care of her chickens and always kept a few. "You never know when you might need eggs, and the meats pretty good as well." Our secret till the reading of the will. And we promised to keep it to ourselves."

She told me how up until the end of WWII her gran and grandfather had lived in India where Walter worked for the government; she didn't know what he did. "It could have been anything," she used to say. "I didn't like to pry. It came with a house so all-in-all life was pretty good. That was up to the end of the war when people were forced to leave. We might have won the war," she said. "We lost the bloody Empire."

"Once home," she continued, "they bought this place. 1948, it was. Round about then. Mum and uncle Ron rebelled at first, both being born abroad. They weren't used to life in Scotland; it was strange. Eventually they settled in okay, and it wasn't long before they left to make a living of their own. Then both got married and had kids. Moved to the city and that was that. Only ever returned occasionally to visit. You know the sort of things, Christmas, and bank holidays. Janine wasn't all that keen on the place. Said it gave her the creeps. It was all in her head of course. I loved it, and still do.

Come on. I want to show you this," she said. Got to her feet then walked to the door that led directly to the kitchen.

"In here to the left," she motioned. "You'll see."

A utility room with a washer and drier, a sink and a banquette seat. Another door with a sign overhead; McEwan's India Pale Ale.

She opened it toward us then reached inside, pulled the cord for light.

Bright.

A wooden staircase led to a cellar twenty feet below, where two large rooms and a cloakroom suite had been built when they put the place up. And I noticed in the first of these, the smaller of the two, as I entered, a sink had been installed along with a two-ring electric hob, and a tiny fridge freezer to make up a small dinette. The larger room was furnished in what I can only describe as typically vintage Indian, and the place smelt heavy of incense. The walls were covered in thangkas and tapestries all with a Buddhist theme.

"I used to love coming down here," she said.

"I spent hours here as a child, taking everything in and trying to figure out what it was about. The questions I had for Walter sounded endless at the time, and probably were. I was an inquisitive child and had a need to know what everything was; why, for, and when? I was intrigued by this other world. And I suppose it was another world in a weird way, given I hadn't been out of the country myself till after he died. I'd immerse myself in his books and objects then probe him as soon as he came in.

Ganesh, he'd say, or Mahakali, goddess of time and death.

It was the zen stuff that got me, even though there wasn't much of it on display. That was kept in the cabinet, under lock and key."

She pointed to a beautiful, hand-painted, armoire depicting the Buddha's feet (Buddhapada).

"And what's the significance of the feet?" I asked, rather intrigued myself.

"They symbolize his presence and absence," she said. "The Buddha. Along with a whole load of other things like non-attachment and Emptiness. At the end of the day that's all any of it really boils down to; Emptiness. That doesn't mean there's nothing there. Things lack a self."

Now my head was beginning to spin. She bent and opened a door.

I peered inside and was met by rows of strange looking books. Titles I hadn't so much as heard of and authors I didn't know existed.

The Blue Cliff Record. The Heart Sutra. The Platform Sutra of the Sixth Patriarch. The Diamond and Three Fold Lotus Sutras.

Bodhidharma, Joshu. Hakuin Ekaku. Vasubandhu and Dogen.

I was lost. Completely out of my depth and I said as much.

"I don't think I'd get my head round any of that. It sounds complicated to me, and I haven't looked inside one of the books yet. The titles are enough to put me off, along with the names of the authors. Hakuin Ekaku? That's a mouthful to begin with, so I can imagine what's inside. What about you, have you read them?" I asked. She probably had.

"Sure," she said. "Well, not exactly read them. More that I've had them explained to me. Walter was always good like that. He'd explain when I asked. This one here." She reached then removed one from the top shelf. "I've lost count of the number of times I've read this one.

Walter always said to forget the rest and concentrate solely on this."

She handed me a copy of The Heart Sutra.

"That gets straight to the heart of the matter without any faffing. Straight to the point and easy to understand. As I said, it's all to do with Emptiness and once you get that everything falls into place. It's not as complicated as it sounds. Everything depends on everything else for its existence - things are neither existent or non-existent, they simply are - and that's what they call Dependent Origination. Everything is always in a state of becoming. Movement. Time."

Christ almighty, my head was swimming, I was going down. Not as complicated as it sounds. Sounded complicated to me.

"Here," she said, as she took the book then sat herself on the sofa; patted a cushion then said to me, "Sit. Sit down here by my side."

I sat on the hand-carved rosewood sofa and positioned a cushion at my back.

She then got up and went into the smaller of the two rooms where I heard her go into the fridge; returned with a bottle of Barr's red cola then sat herself back down.

"So, The Heart Sutra. Or to give it its Sanskrit title, Mahaprajnaparamitahridaya, which translates as, The Heart of the Perfection of Wisdom."

Easy. Not too complicated, that's what she said. I was in a maze. This was going to hurt my brain, I could tell that straight away.

She went on.

"The noble Avalokiteshvara bodhisattva whilst practicing the deep practice of prajnaparamita looked upon the five Skandhas and seeing they were empty of self-existence said …"

"Wow," I said, with a hand to stop her. "You told me it wasn't complicated."

"Not so much as it sounds."

"Avalowhatever and bodhiskandhas. Sounds complicated to me."

"Avalokiteshvara," she said. "is the compassionate side of Buddha's nature and takes the form of Guanyin in East Asian Buddhism. And a Bodhisattva is someone who is on the path to Buddhahood but renounces it until they have saved all others. In earlier texts the term was used to refer to Siddhartha Gautama himself."

"Who?"

"Buddha. That was his name. Siddhartha Gautama. Buddha."

"Ah."

She then went on with her reading of the text after she'd explained Shariputra to me.

"Here, Shariputra, form is Emptiness, Emptiness is form. Form is not separate from Emptiness, Emptiness is not separate from form. Whatever is form is Emptiness, whatever is Emptiness is form. The same holds for sensation, perception, volition, and consciousness. Here, Shariputra, all dharmas are marked by Emptiness, not by purity or impurity, increase or decrease, birth or annihilation."

She filled two glasses with the Barr's red cola then handed one to me.

"Therefore, Shariputra, in Emptiness there is no form, sensation, perception, volition or consciousness. No eye, no ear, no nose, no tongue, no body, no mind. No shape, no sound, no smell, no taste, no feeling, no thought. There is no realm of sight, through to no realm of cognition. There is no ignorance or ending of ignorance, through to no aging and death or ending of aging and death. There is no suffering, no cause of suffering, no ending of suffering and no path. There is no wisdom and no attainment."

She laid the book on the table, facedown, then asked if it made any sense.

"Is it making any sense, or do you find it a bit of a grind?"

"I'm getting the gist. I think I'm keeping up."

"Good. So long as you remember it's dealing with a lack of inherent existence in things, you'll be fine. Mind and the Alya-vijnana we'll leave to another day. There's enough in here to keep you going as there is. Well, there's actually nothing to be honest with you," she laughed, then continued to read.

"Therefore, Shariputra, with nothing to attain, bodhisattvas, relying on prajnaparamita, have no obstructions in their minds. Without obstructions, they have no fear. Far beyond inverted views and dreams, they reach the ultimate nirvana. All buddhas appearing in the past, present and future rely on prajnaparamita and realise perfect enlightenment, anattura-samyak-sambodhi."

I listened intently, deciding not to open my mouth and stay quiet till the end.

"Therefore, know that prajnaparamita is the great mantra of wisdom, the mantra of great clarity, the unsurpassed mantra, the unequalled mantra which removes all suffering. It is true, not false. Recite the mantra of prajnaparamita: Gate gate paragate parasamgate bodhi svaha."

I looked with the question, Is that you finished?

She looked back and simply said, "Done." Closed the book, put it back on the shelf, then shut the armoire door.

"Sorry about that. It always gets to me. I feel I've got to read it to the end before I can put it down. We'll give mind and the Alya-vijnana a miss if the look on your face is anything to go by, what do you think?"

I replied, "I think we will." Then left the thing at that.

Emptiness?

6

We moved in at the beginning of spring and once again I had changed jobs and was now working in a small engineering plant as a press operator, seven out of seven, trying to get cash together so we could go on our travels.

We hadn't been 'away' as we liked to call it in over a year, and even at that it was only a four day stay with friends of Joyce's who lived in a renovated barn they'd converted in the town of Lannion in the department of Brittany, northwest France with the intention of turning it into a commune for the likes of artists and writers.

And it was here we first made the acquaintance of Jules and Lena, two really crazy German cranks, living way out on the edge.

"Today, Lena, I paint one of Hitler using my cock and balls. Only my cock and balls, Lena. Only my cock and balls."

They were constantly drunk - and naked, the place having been advertised as a naturist establishment from the onset - although their level of drunkenness was never blotto. A steady, kept-at-a-level, simmering away drunk. Working their way through bottle after bottle of merlot from early morning till late at night. Usually starting with a glass in hand and a croissant or two for breakfast.

He'd then jump up and dance, waving his arms in the air.

"Today I paint the Hindenburg disaster, Lena, Straight off of Led Zeppelin one. Cock and balls, Lena. Only cock and balls."

It was always, "Today I paint, Lena," whatever the hell it was. And it was always whatever he conjured up over breakfast while Lena worked away at whatever she was working on at the time.

"Jules, listen to this," she'd occasionally say, then read from the top of the page.

"Is it really any wonder
when the boys all swing the lead
and the girls stay up drinking
and the wine goes to their head
that when they get up in the morning
crawl hungover from their bed
that they have fresh fried tomatoes
with their cheese and scrambled egg.
*That they have fresh fried tomatoes
with their cheese and scrambled egg."*

These would be broadcast to whoever was listening; mostly for the benefit of Jules.

David and Rosa, having heard it all before, merely went about their business making sure the guests had enough to eat and drink, and that anything they required was supplied.

"Eh, what do you think Jules? What do you think? This one hits the mark?"

Jules already had his cock in the paint, splashing it onto the page.

"Today I paint a nice one of the Eifel Tower, Lena. Only with the cock and balls. Ha. Only the cock and balls."

Then she'd be off with her next piece of writing, ink hardly dry on the page.

"Jules, what do you think about this I write? You like this one, or no?"

Jules sits down on the edge of a lounger a glass of wine in hand.

"I listen," he says, then takes a drink, lights a cigarette.

"Crones with no teeth in a shaky cartoon
fill a cauldron way up to the brim
when a couple of brothers arrive on the scene
and watch them drop babies in.
Said Jacob to Wilhelm, as it bubbled away,
 'Should we show this one back in Berlin?'
Said Wilhelm to Jacob, 'I've gave up the ghost.
I think it's a wee bit too Grimm.'"

Jules perked up and said he liked it. Liked it very much. "Yes."

"Now, Jeff and Joyce, you must come see my wonderful painting of Der Führer. No?"

This we had to see. Painted with cock and balls?

Shit, it looked like a representation of Frank Zappa straight from the cover of Cruising With Ruben and the Jets, right on down to the beak, which, as soon as I laid eyes on it, I took to have been painted with his cock. I loved it, and Joyce was of the same opinion.

We bought it there on the spot for five, and it hangs to this day in our kitchen.

Signed with the nom de plume *Cockerball,* it always makes us smile.

The Zeppelin one was not for sale. He was keeping that one for himself.

We met a lot like this, and I slowly became accustomed to the wanton madness innate in most of the people she introduced me to. I half expected it, and on the odd occasion I made the acquaintance of one of her 'normal' friends I'd wonder what ailed then bide my time in the expectation that madness would soon ensue.

With some it didn't, with most it did, and those were the ones I loved.

The crazies. The mad, up for anything type that you didn't have to ask twice to dress in women's clothing or vice versa who didn't mind making a fool of themselves or if they did were quite unaware they were doing so. Caught in the moment of whatever it was they were caught in the moment doing.

And it wasn't always her friends. She collected crazies like others collect collectables.

Like the time we arrived in Zürich at two in the morning having come in by train from Innsbruck.

We'd been travelling on one of those student train ticket deals where you purchase a rail card that affords you up to one month unlimited travel on the various rail networks throughout Europe and had set out to have quite a time.

A British Rail ferry across the channel then onward down toward Paris where we did the usual touristy type things and took in the Arc de Triomphe, the Eifel Tower, Montmartre and then the Louvre.

We were camping, so the need to find hotel accommodation was non-existent, and we quickly discovered a pitch at Camping Le Transat 14 RdPt des Champs Elysées-Marcel Dassault, 75008 Paris, where we happily spent the next three days before heading further south.

It was only a place to lay our heads, so during the day we were free.

We hit the bars and explored the city, eating on the hoof as we went.

This suited us, as any form of regimentation that was likely to be inflicted upon us, had we decided to book a hotel room beforehand, would have seriously impinged on the free-style travelling we envisaged before setting out.

The idea was to set up camp in a location that suited our temperament, then once happy with the lay of the land, eat and drink on the hoof till we made up our minds it was time to move, always with an eye to the coast.

Breakfast eight to ten in a grubby hotel dining room then evening meal from six to nine didn't appeal.

The idea was to travel as freely as we could and restrictions such as being told when to eat your meals then check out in the morning - ten till twelve - didn't make any sense. Not the way we figured it. That was for Mr and Mrs. People that like to eat and drink at specific junctures of day. Suited and booted for seven at night; down for the evening meal. Two glass of wine then twice round the floor. A tribute act then bed.

Shit.

Three days later we were on the move, headed toward Marseille.

We'd taken a late SNCF from Gare de Lyon and were happy to share the compartment with four Swedes heading in the same direction, and with about as much regard for convention as we had at the time. Then after initial introductions the seats were slid out together, and the armrests lifted to form what became in effect a king size bed.

All aboard. We spent our journey getting drunk and singing songs.

Botvid and Hilding on acoustic guitars, the girls and myself drumming packs.

The wine flowed freely along with the beer, and the consequences that brought - as if we didn't know - inevitably caused us to get drunk.

And we did.

Next thing I knew we were bound for Nice, Marseille nothing more than a blot on the landscape, disappearing off to our rear.

"What happened there?" I asked, confused and perplexed in equal measure at having not seen the place, or not remembering having done so. It was useless.

Joyce was as bewildered and dumb struck as I was, and as she sat there with the old bobble head rattling along in time to the train, I had to dig her in the ribs.

"Hoe. Happened there?" I said, with a dig. "How did we end up here?"

She sat up straight, then sorted herself. Pulled herself together.

"What?"

She rubbed her eyes then glanced through the window, the countryside moving at speed.

"Where are we headed for now?" she asked, truly unaware.

"Well, according to the ticket collector, ten minutes ago, we're heading in the direction of Nice."

"Nice?"

"That's what he said. The 05.32 from Marseille. We arrive at half past eight. He stamped our cards then left. Nice enough guy."

Twenty minutes later we were standing on the concourse of Gare de Nice-Ville wondering what the hell was next.

Last I remembered was alighting the train with our Swedish friends in Marseille, then after that a blank.

According to Joyce we hit the bars and kept drinking till ten or eleven at night when our new-found companions said their goodbyes and left, saying they had places and people to see, and they'd definitely keep in touch.

It reminded her of a Welfare trip to Burntisland, when as a child she'd go with her parents only to spend the day in pubs while they got out of their minds. Back on the bus at closing time, loaded with a carry-out.

"From there," she said, "we went back to the station where we slept on the concourse floor, as any attempt to find a place to pitch the tent in the state we were in, was out of the question. And as you were in no fit state to decide one way or another, I made it for us. As to how we ended up here, I haven't a clue."

"Ah, that was me when I woke this morning. I bought the tickets from the booth. Getting you on board was difficult, though I managed it fine in the end."

Rough?

Rough as badger's arses. We had to get back on track. And the first thing to do was find a place to pitch the tent and rest. A night of drunken sleep in a station had seriously shattered our nerves. This being Nice, a place to pitch was proving an impossible task.

It was our own fault.

We hadn't bothered discussing logistics before setting off as we took it for granted we'd jump on a train and end up in a town with a campsite; Pitches available. Minimum stay three nights.

The only place we had made provision for was the army camp at Rheindahlen, Germany, where we'd arranged to visit an old friend I'd gone to school with and who was now serving in the R.C.T. and had been stationed there these past three month. And all going well, that was to be our last port of call before we made for home.

Things were pressing, and we had to camp.

We shouldered our packs then started to tramp, looking for information.

Tourist.

They informed us we'd have to go back to St. Lauren du Var. A Madame Clement, they said, who allowed the occasional camper the use of the land to the rear of her house next to her half dozen gites. Easy enough to find, they said, then marked it out on a map.

Two hours later we were glad of the pitch and set about throwing up the tent. We made ourselves a bite to eat, then fell asleep in our bags.

By the time we woke the sun had gone so we studied the map by flash.

Joyce fingered Venice. "There," she said. "Then on to Lido de Jesolo. Lie in the sun a day or two then make our way back north."

I wasn't of a mind to offer resistance and lying in the sun held sway.

Two days of relaxation suited me down to the ground.

The two days we'd initially pencilled in to spend in the sun turned into six. Soaked in grappa in the pit of our tent, only ever leaving to ablute; re-supply our dwindling food stock, shit, piss, and buy booze.

Grappa.

Grappa, grappa, grappa, grappa. Grappa, grappa, grappa.

What the hell was this stuff? We didn't have a clue.

"The Devil's peepee," proffered Joyce. I could only nod my head.

Hit you like a sledgehammer, straight to the forehead, then spun you inside the tent. Opened the flaps then fired you out, lying there buckled in the sand.

The grapes looked nice on the label, before we started in hard. Deceptive. The stuff was downright lethal. You could have fuelled fighter jets on the stuff or sent a rocket to the moon. The bottle should have carried a warning on the side: Drink at one's own risk. It didn't. We considered suing the makers for damages, damages to liver and lungs. The poison had hardened our livers to rock whilst the vapour had scarred our lungs. Scarred them to the point that if one had looked - a specialist in diseases of such - they'd have diagnosed mesothelioma.

"Ever work with asbestos?" they'd ask. A look of concern on their faces. "Grappa?"

"Grappa," we'd reply … "In the mid to late seventies … Italy … Lido de Jesolo."

The cool mountain air we breathed on arrival in Innsbruck felt like an extra strong mint. And stepping from the train we gulped it in, five and a half litres at a time. Enough to re-generate our ravaged systems then set us once more on our way.

Zürich.

Next calling point on our trip of adventure that was giving us the endless shakes. Suffering from alcohol use disorder we didn't even know we had.

"Hi, Richard Klein," I heard the voice as we stood there drinking at the bar.

"I'll get those," he said with a smile, then paid the barman in full.

"English?"

I looked at him standing there, five foot-four, in a pair of Cuban heels.

"Scottish," I told him, as we lifted our drinks, thanked him, then walked away. We were headed for the table in the corner by the fire where we sat down to take off the weight.

He followed on slowly at our backs; sat down. "Scottish? You know Jim Baxter?"

I nearly choked on my lager and couldn't believe my ears.

It was par for the course that whichever country you visited - once you cleared up the issue of nationality and declared that under no circumstances you were English or were ever likely to be - and made known you were a member of the Scottish race, then you had to be acquainted with so-and-so or their brother.

Did they think the country was the size of a postage stamp, and the inhabitants living in close proximity?

Huh. Jim Baxter, indeed. Up my fucking arse.

I asked anyway.

"Jim Baxter, the football player?" I said. "Is that the person you mean?"

Joyce looked on with complete disinterest, football wasn't her bag.

It wasn't mine either, however I knew enough from time spent growing up with a mixed marriage family, on my mother's side, to know the name Jim Baxter, and that he played for Glasgow Rangers, never to be spoken of in front of granda James. That was a no-no and likely to see you banished to the kitchen till you'd learned to control your tongue, and he'd cooled down sufficiently to allow you back in the living room.

"Don't mention that name again," he'd say, as he pulled on his pipe.

"Fucking, Jim Baxter. Couldn't lace Jinky's boots. Neither could Wullie Henderson."

Then my uncle would shoot straight back with a retort like, "Yer arse … No in the same fucking league."

Our German friend insisted it was Baxter. "Played for Rangers and Scotland at the time," he said.

"We met when I was working as part of the physio team at Real Madrid, and we played Rangers at Ibrox in September 63.

The score ended up one nil to us. Then after the match, Baxter invited Puskas to a party in Easterhouse and I tagged along. Puskas scored again that night, making it two in a row."

Joyce drew me a look then lifted an eyebrow. She had always attracted them. Nuts.

And this guy was.

He told us he was friends with Frank Sinatra and Sammy Davis Jr., and had partied with them on a trip to Las Vegas. He wasn't sure how he came to be in their company in the first place, he said; Maybe through staying at The Sands.

Shit.

Next thing he told us he was living it up with Salvidor Dali in Spain.

The guy was a gasbag, and the drunker he got the more outlandish he became. And he didn't disappoint. He ended up on the floor dancing with himself. Doing The Twist and The Mashed Potato. The Wah Watusi and The Skate.

We were in hysterics and suspected this was his normal behaviour after a belly-full of beer. We could have gone and left him to it. However, having been privy to this type of behaviour from certain individuals within our own sphere of friends for as long as we cared to remember we were in no hurry to vacate the premises and move on. Besides, we had nowhere to go, and the idea of spending another night on a cold, drafty concourse out on a railroad station didn't exactly fill us with joy. On the contrary. Another night on a cold tiled floor was likely to do me in. And I was aware from speaking with Joyce, earlier in the day, she felt the same.

So, staying put was our only choice.

And the entertainment was free.

We'd only scraped the surface when the sun came up in the sky.

Grace Kelly.

Barbara Streisand.

Groucho Marx.

The Beatles.

He was sitting in his pants, black shoes and socks, by the time we vacated the place. Slumped on his seat like a buckled bin, totally, completely exhausted.

Bacon, sausage,
fried egg.
   Yogacara
in your head.
   Inherent nature
never led
     permeating all.

We were on another train, thundering toward Düsseldorf, stuffing our faces with Meitschibie and drinking Eichhof beer.

We were settled, and as the journey was expected to last five and a half hours, we'd removed our shoes for comfort. We'd purchased a number of magazines, in English, from the concourse shop, and with an empty compartment we were free to lounge as we pleased.

We fell asleep and when I opened my eyes Düsseldorf came into view.

I gave Joyce a shake then we both pulled our packs from the overhead racking above.

Any hope of respite, we may have been harbouring, from the mayhem ensued on our journey so far was short lived. Charlie was waiting to greet us on the concourse and whisk us off for fun.

Rheindahlen.

It was an army camp for god's sake. What the hell did we expect? Sun-loungers by the pool and a never-ending flow of pina coladas? Well, if that were the case, we'd have been sorely disappointed. More like non-stop dancing and drinking, pints of Asbach and coke.

The Blue Lagoon was a hotbed of iniquity, squaddies without control.

A week of this and we were glad at last to reach the port at Ostend.

We were truly happy when we boarded the ferry and finally cast off for home.

We didn't. We made for Kent instead.

We were skint. And the only place I could come up with to get money to make the trip north was an aunt on my father's side who lived in a small village in the Kent countryside and who I knew would help us out, put us up for two or three days before she'd send us on our way. A real gem of a woman who'd give up her bed for us and sleep on the couch for however long we stayed. Give us the money for the journey home and fill us up with booze.

We'd be made more than welcome by herself and her husband. Made to feel at home.

And we were.

Hot baths and mountains of food, liquor from the cupboard on tap.

Four days later we pulled into Waverley, sated beyond belief.

It was good to be home, and the first thing I did was look for new employment.

I was fed-up working the press at Clarke's and fancied a change. A job I could get my teeth into rather than standing there pulling a lever, feeling the monotony kill me.

I was bored to tears, and anything surely was better than this; Day in pulling that lever.

I hadn't searched long when a job came up, courtesy of Uncle Bert. Spray-painting trucks on an automated line, working in the B.L. Plant.

I was in.

Then a strange thing happened; Joyce started hoarding food. Small things at first like tins of Fray Bentos steak and kidney pies, corned beef and beans.

She bought a camp stove, and canisters of gas then stored them in the cupboard by the sink.

Week by week she added to the pile like a prepper awaiting the bomb.

Toilet rolls, disinfectant, dried pasta and rice. Peanut butter, popcorn, dried fruit and sugar.

She must have bought every canned meat there was.

Chilli con carne, potted meat, Goblin burgers, Spam.

It was all there, and over the weeks it grew to gigantic proportions, almost filling the room.

Lentils and tubs of powdered milk. Boiled sweets and honey.

It got to the point I had to ask her what was going on. It was bugging me. I had to know.

"Hey, Joyce," I said, as she came in with more tins, "what's with the food in the cellar?"

She went into the kitchen and dropped the bags, sat herself on a chair.

"Well," she said. "The last three year have been tough, and the prospect of living through another like seventy-three, seventy-four when the miners and railroad workers were on strike and the government put us on a three-day week and restricted our electricity use scares me to death, if you must know.

All was in a state of darkness, what with one strike after another, and not much light at the end of the tunnel unless you happened to have access to candles and were prepared to light them whenever they felt like cutting the electricity, and that was near enough daily.

We were reduced to drinking bottled beer in the pub, and it's the prospect of living through a time like that again terrifies me and is causing me a bit of anxiety. That's why I'm buying the food," she said. "I'd like to be prepared. A security blanket. It was pretty out-there last time, and next time it might be worse. And if we don't get rid of this labour government, I've a feeling I might be correct."

I was confused so sat down beside her. I didn't understand any of it as politics wasn't my thing and was never likely to be, along with football or golf. And the more I tried to get a grasp of what she was saying about the three-day week and blackouts and shit like that the more it escaped my mind.

What if we did revert to times like that? We'd come out of it like we had before; none the worse for ware. We always came out of whatever difficulty we happened to find ourselves in. And I didn't see the future being any way different. I didn't see a problem. There again I never did. I took things as they came and to hell with the consequences.

"It's better we have a supply. You never know what might come."

And I didn't. I didn't have a clue as to what was about to happen as the balls I had were hairy and in no way made of crystal. And when I said that to her, she shook her head and said, "See, that's your problem."

And it was. And I knew it was. What did we have to worry about in the great scheme of things, really? Nothing as far as I could see. We'd a roof over our heads that was fully paid and without small children to look out for, life was pretty plain sailing.

"Never take anything serious. That's you. Always a laugh and joke. One of these days you won't be laughing with this lot we have in power. You'll see. Bringing the country to its knees. A bunch of lefties."

"What? … A bunch of lefties?"

That was the sort of thing I'd never get: A bunch of lefties.

If I lived a thousand years, I don't think I'd get it. It baffled me.

How could anyone who'd spent time at a CND peace camp and taken part in a half-dozen demonstrations possibly complain about a Labour government and call them a bunch of lefties? I was bamboozled. It didn't fit. And the more I got to know Joyce, lots of things didn't fit. She was a mass of contradictions, like things could be true and false at the same time and how everything is in the process of becoming its opposite.

My brain was scrambled, and each time she spoke about zen, I felt a scream coming on.

She'd say, as if I were interested, things like, "Everything that exists is without being because everything exists without existing in conventional terms."

I considered I'd been getting along with The Heart Sutra, making progress, after further readings, when she opened up with a broadside and started to go off in tangents. I was lost and felt I could melt.

"Things only exist in a changing state and by means of change. Underlying all change is potentiality. Mujo," she'd say. "Impermanence. Everything is empty and impermanent. This is because that is. This is not because that is not."

I still didn't understand how she functioned in the head.

Lefties?

No doubt there was something there, if I'd only taken time to consider matters. She'd a second sight for things that were about to take place and was always on about the direction they'd take, and likely outcome. And she was usually on point. The Winter of Discontent a prime example.

"A tyrant," she'd say. "That's what we'll get. A tyrant at the end of this."

And as it transpired it was a winter of discontent, what with one thing and another. Then when the workers at Ford finally settled for a seventeen per cent pay increase - twelve per cent above the limit set by the government - people surmised that was that.

Was it hell as like.

The main course was yet to come, along with dessert and cheese board.

The haulage workers were next to have a go - no doubt in the assumption that if the government had caved to the demands of workers in a car factory, then they'd be in with a shout.

Mayhem prevailed, and before we knew what was happening gravediggers also had a bone to grind and threw their tools in a hole.

Refuse workers joined their ranks; bodies and trash piled high.

"It doesn't seem that nonsensical now," said Joyce, "does it; the hoarding of food?"

She opened the Sun at the middle pages then spread it out on the table.

"It says here." she said, taking a puff at a cigarette she'd lit, "that NHS auxiliary workers are thinking of coming out next. Fuck. They shouldn't have put a cap on wage rises," she said. "They've only got themselves to blame. Who the fuck does this Callaghan think he is, or what he is, untouchable? Next thing you know he'll be telling us there's nothing to worry about, and there isn't any crisis. It's alright for him to go lolling about in the sun. The rest of us have got to stay here and suck it up. "Lefties, Jeff, I'm telling you. A bunch of bloody lefties. Next thing you know they'll be blaming the press for making the whole thing up. I wouldn't trust any of them as far as I could throw them. A bunch of fucking cunts."

She was off on one and no mistake, so I let her ramble on.

She'd probably be at it for the next half hour till she finally ran out of steam.

That was usually how things worked: she usually ran out of steam. Gave up the ghost then changed the subject.

She was right, however. The country was being run into the ground by a bunch of lefties. They were bringing it to its knees, the government and unions alike. Drastic measures needed to be taken to get it back on its feet.

She'd said Callaghan was deluded. Surely we couldn't go back to a conservative government even considering Thatcher, an unknown quantity, we couldn't go back to that. Could we?

I went to our storeroom for two Fray Bentos pies then popped them into the oven.

Tinned potatoes, a tin of peas, Bisto gravy and tea.

By six o'clock we were all on the sofa watching the strikes on the news.

"Salt?"

*

BOOK TWO

*

The Soviet army's Red Star journal named her the Iron Lady.

1

And it came to pass on the fourth of May the Jabberwocky arrived.

> *'Twas brillig, and the slithy toves*
> *Did gyre and gimble in the wabe:*
> *All mimsy were the borogoves,*
> *And the mome raths outgrabe.*
>
> *"Beware the Jabberwock, my son!*
> *The jaws that bite, the claws that catch!*
> *Beware the Jubjub bird, and shun*
> *The frumious Bandersnatch!"*
>
> *He took his vorpal sword in hand;*
> *Long time the manxome foe he sought—*
> *So rested he by the Tumtum tree*
> *And stood awhile in thought.*
>
> *And, as in uffish thought he stood,*
> *The Jabberwock, with eyes of flame,*
> *Came whiffling through the tulgey wood,*
> *And burbled as it came!*
>
> *One, two! One, two! And through and through*
> *The vorpal blade went snicker-snack!*
> *He left it dead, and with its head*
> *He went galumphing back.*

"And hast thou slain the Jabberwock?
Come to my arms, my beamish boy!
O frabjous day! Callooh! Callay!"
He chortled in his joy.

'Twas brillig, and the slithy toves
Did gyre and gimble in the wabe:
All mimsy were the borogoves,
And the mome raths outgrabe.*

"The lady is not for turning.
The lady is not for turning.
The lady is not for turning.
The lady is not for turning."

She puzzled over this, then suddenly was struck by brainwave.

Grind them into the ground with madness then disappear into the night.

A thrilling remembrance, if nothing else, of happy summer days.

"I knew this would happen," Joyce thought out loud. And I knew right away what she meant.

She was on about Thatcher and the new Tory government that had displaced Callaghan's mob in a general election and were now in charge of the country.

"It's not going to end well," she said. "Mark my words. A woman in charge of the country? That's all we need; a mad-ass bitch who thinks she can run the show where others have failed. She's already taken milk from seven to eleven-year-olds then had the audacity to argue the point she was only carrying on from where Labour left off, as they'd been the ones who'd stopped its allocation in secondary schools. Can you believe that? Really? And people voted for her? I find that hard to believe. I really do. I knew things were bad under the last lot, but a woman - and especially her - I ask you; whatever the hell will be next? A marionette? Nothing surprises me now. And I truly believe that. Milk."

Once again, she'd hit me with bamboozle and put my mind in a spin.

It was confusing enough when I'd heard her rail against Callaghan and his Labour government the way she had by calling them a bunch of lefties. That I didn't expect, and coming out of the blue the way it had, hitting me broadside, came as a bit of a shock. However, this - purposely decrying a woman in power - was different. Especially when spouted with venom. And her criterion for judging in such a harsh manner I couldn't fathom. "Because I can," she'd say, then leave it at that.

She walked to the record player then dropped the needle on, Moanin' by Charlie Mingus.

"I think the plug's been pulled," she said. "And we're rushing toward the hole. And I don't imagine, for one minute, any amount of effort to cling to the rim is likely to save us. Do you?"

I was stumped and said the first thing that entered my mind. Which wasn't usually the correct thing.

"I was thinking you'd be happy to have a woman in power. Level up the field."

She drew me a look and I read her face, which more than said it all. She was het:

The Mock Turtle sighed deeply, and drew the back of one flapper across his eyes. He looked at Alice and tried to speak, but for a minute or two sobs choked his voice. "Same as if he had a bone in his throat," said the Gryphon, and it set to work shaking him and punching him in the back. At last the Mock Turtle recovered his voice, and, with tears running down his cheeks, he went on again: -

"You may not have lived much under the sea -" ("I haven't," said Alice) -"and perhaps you were never even introduced to a lobster -" (Alice began to say "I once tasted -" but checked herself hastily, and said, "No, never") "- so you can have no idea what a delightful thing a Lobster-Quadrille is!"

"No, indeed," said Alice. "What sort of a dance is it?"

"Why," said the Gryphon, "you first form into a line along the sea-shore -"

"Two lines!" cried the Mock Turtle. "Seals, turtles, salmon, and so on: then, when you've cleared all the jelly-fish out of the way -"

"That generally takes some time," interrupted the Gryphon.

"- you advance twice -"

"Each with a lobster as a partner!" cried the Gryphon.

"Of course," the Mock Turtle said: "advance twice, set to partners -"

"- change lobsters, and retire in the same order," continued the Gryphon.

"Then, you know," the Mock Turtle went on, *"you throw the -"*

"The lobsters!" shouted the Gryphon, with a bound into the air.

"- as far out to sea as you can -"

"Swim after them!" screamed the Gryphon.

"Turn a somersault in the sea!" cried the Mock Turtle, capering wildly about.

"Change lobsters again!" yelled the Gryphon at the top of its voice.

"Back to land again, and - that's all the first figure," said the Mock Turtle, suddenly dropping his voice; and the two creatures, who had been jumping about like mad things all this time, sat down again very sadly and quietly, and looked at Alice.

"It must be a very pretty dance," said Alice timidly.

"Would you like to see a little of it?" said the Mock Turtle.

"Very much indeed," said Alice.

"Come, let's try the first figure!" said the Mock Turtle to the Gryphon. *"We can do it without lobsters, you know. Which shall sing?"*

"Oh, you sing," said the Gryphon. *"I've forgotten the words."*

So they began solemnly dancing round and round Alice, every now and then treading on her toes when they passed too close, and waving their forepaws to mark the time, while the Mock Turtle sang this, very slowly and sadly: -

"Will you walk a little faster?" said a whiting to a snail,
"There's a porpoise close behind us, and he's treading on my tail.
See how eagerly the lobsters and the turtles all advance!
They are waiting on the shingle - will you come and join the dance?
Will you, won't you, will you, won't you, will you join the dance?
Will you, won't you, will you, won't you, won't you join the dance?

"You can really have no notion how delightful it will be
When they take us up and throw us, with the lobsters, out to sea!"
But the snail replied, "Too far, too far!" and gave a look askance -
Said he thanked the whiting kindly, but he would not join the dance.
   Would not, could not, would not, could not, would not join the dance.
   Would not, could not, would not, could not, could not join the dance.

"What matters it how far we go?" his scaly friend replied,
"There is another shore, you know, upon the other side.
The further off from England the nearer is to France -

Then turn not pale, beloved snail, but come and join the dance.
Will you, won't you, will you, won't you, will you join the dance?
Will you, won't you, will you, won't you, won't you join the dance?"*

"They can forget that, Jeff. If they think I'm about to join their dance they've got another think coming. And that's all I'm saying on the matter. They can all go take a fuck. It was one thing trying to make ends meet under a bunch of socialist like we had before. I'm telling you, Jeff, with the Tories in power, it's about to get ten times worse. They attracted votes from the National Front. What the hell does that tell you?"

She had a point. I suspected Thatcher to be divisive, and madness to ensue once she'd been in a while. I couldn't, for the life of me, see any other outcome in the long term the way things stood. Drastic measures were required if things were to be righted, and for most of the population, who up until now were more than satisfied with the status quo, it would be a bitter pill to swallow.

If we wished to get the country back on its feet, poison may have to be administered, and as witches are dab-hands at that particular potion, Thatcher was the lady for the job.

Huh!

It was all very well to say "Drink me," but the wise little Alice was not going to do that in a hurry. "No, I'll look first," she said, "and see whether it's *marked 'poison' or not"; for she had read several nice little histories about children who had got burnt, and eaten up by wild beasts and other unpleasant things, all because they would not remember the simple rules their friends had taught them: such as, that a red-hot poker will burn you if you hold it too long; and that if you cut your finger very deeply with a knife, it usually bleeds; and she had never forgotten that, if you drink much from a bottle marked 'poison,' it is almost certain to disagree with you, sooner or later.**

Curiouser and curiouser. Curiouser and Curiouser. Things were getting madder by the minute.

2

Things were about to get a whole lot worse; in more ways than I'd considered.

It was a Friday as I recall and we'd sat down to a late breakfast, or 'brunch,' when who should come to the door but Janine: the last person we expected to see. And as she stood there with a face like fizz, I was in two minds whether or not to let her in, then relented almost immediately and showed her into the kitchen - having her walk behind me at a dutiful number of paces - albeit she knew the way well enough herself.

I wanted her to seethe a while longer before she got to Joyce. Because whatever the nature of her visit may be, it wouldn't be anything nice. Nothing that'd bring joy to our lives or crack a smile on our lips. That's for sure.

And Janine being Janine, as she always was, was unlikely to disappoint.

"Don't you think it's time you got that phone of yours connected?" she said, as soon as she stepped in the kitchen, taking Joyce by surprise.

This time there was nowhere I could possibly go save the garden. I stayed.

"What?"

"The phone," she said. Time you got it connected. It's been out of commission since gran died and you haven't bothered your arse."

Joyce stood up and squared her off.

"What the hell do you want?"

"For a start, get your phone connected. That way I wouldn't have to make the journey to see you in person when things happen, and we feel the need to inform you. Having said that, I wouldn't have bothered myself if it hadn't been for mum. She's the one said you should be told, so here I am in person."

"Well say what you've got to say," said Joyce, then close the door when you leave."

"It's auntie Sargent," she said with a grin. "She died this morning at three."

Joyce went stiff, grabbed the back of a chair, turned it then sat herself down.

"What?"

"Auntie Sargent," repeated Janine. "She died this morning.

She'd been ill for a time," she then went on. "Cancer in her head and neck."

I looked to Joyce and could see she was dumbstruck, sitting with her head in her hands. Janine had pulled the rug from her feet, and she'd hit the floor with a bang.

"Why was I not informed she was ill? You know what she meant to me."

"You'd have been informed," retorted Janine, "if only you'd connected your phone."

"Connected the phone," spat Joyce, in reply. "That's a poor excuse. Connect the phone. You're only a bloody hour away, if that, and you leave it till now before coming to see me; when she's dead. You could have had the decency to let me know she was ill. It's another way of getting at me, isn't it? You're sick, Janine, and you always have been. Anything to hurt and you're on it. Especially where it concerns me. You're sick, Janine, and think it's fun to have people suffer. I often wondered about your lack of friends growing up. I should have put two and two together to get the answer to that one. And nothing has changed: You're still friendless. You'll go to your grave a horrible, miserable old woman. No one there. Buried all on your own. With a bit of luck that bastard your married to will still be alive; other than that, you're on your own. Because no way I'll be there.

Now close the door on your way out, and *don't* come back."

I hadn't seen Joyce in this state before. Although well I could understand it.

I didn't know auntie Sargent. I felt I did.

She was an aunt on the paternal side and had joined the Wrens in the late fifties, climbing through the ranks where she gained the position of Chief Officer and served out fifteen year, coming home on leave when she could to spend time with family and friends.

And it was these times Joyce recalled with fondness.

Gaze.

"I remember;" she would always start a story, then weave things on from there.

Like the time she told me of her coming home in uniform - double-breasted jacket and skirt, white shirt and black tie with a tricorne hat on top - and taking her straight to the Kelvin Hall: carnival time at Christmas.

"We rode the dodgems and speedway," she said. "Saw elephants, tigers and lions.

I was only a child at the time. It's seared in my memory."

She tapped her temple with her middle finger, rapidly, then drew a face.

"And that bitch comes to tell me she's dead. She knew what she was doing. I hope to fuck she rots in hell, even if that's too good.

We won a goldfish. Didn't last a week."

I knew the stories and understood from what I'd been told exactly what Joyce must be feeling.

She loved auntie Sargent, and to hear of her passing in the manner she had - from a sister who'd done all she could to belittle and bring her down - must have been a crushing blow. And I knew it.

I knew of the time she'd taken her to Blackpool and up to the top of the tower. Then in to see the rock being made, candyfloss and dogs.

The gifts she'd brought her from overseas and the movies she'd taken her to see.

She'd taken her aboard ship when docked at Rosyth, where the sailors on board made a helluva fuss over her and she left eleven pound richer.

They were great times, and she'd often tell me stories related to her - when she was older and better equipped to understand - of auntie's time in foreign ports, living it up with her friends:

Drinks by the Grand Harbour in Malta.
Gibraltar and the Falkland Islands.
Then it suddenly started to dawn as news came over the radio.

Who would buy stolen words from a thief?
You would?
You would?
Who would buy stolen words from a thief?
You would?
You would?
You would?
Who would buy stolen words from a thief?
You would?
You would?
Who would buy stolen words from a thief?
You would?
You would?
You would?

For as to what we have heard you affirm, that there are other kingdoms and states in the world inhabited by human creatures as large as yourself, our philosophers are in much doubt, and would rather conjecture that you dropped from the moon, or one of the stars; because it is certain, that a hundred mortals of your bulk would in a short time destroy all the fruits and cattle of his majesty's dominions: besides, our histories of six thousand moons make no mention of any other regions than the two great empires of Lilliput and Blefuscu. Which two mighty powers have, as I was going to tell you, been engaged in a most obstinate war for six–and–thirty moons past. It began upon the following occasion. It is allowed on all hands, that the primitive way of breaking eggs, before we eat them, was upon the larger end; but his present majesty's grandfather, while he was a boy, going to eat an egg, and breaking it according to the ancient practice, happened to cut one of his fingers. Whereupon the emperor his father published an edict, commanding all his subjects, upon great penalties, to break the smaller end of their eggs. The people so highly resented this law, that our histories tell us, there have been six rebellions raised on that account; wherein one emperor lost his life, and another his crown. These civil commotions were constantly fomented by the monarchs of Blefuscu; and when they were quelled, the exiles always fled for refuge to that empire. It is computed that eleven thousand persons have at several times suffered death, rather than submit to break their eggs at the smaller end. Many hundred large volumes have been published upon this controversy: but the books of the Big–endians have been long forbidden, and the whole party rendered incapable by law of holding employments. During the course of these troubles, the emperors of Blefusca did frequently expostulate by their ambassadors, accusing us of making a schism in religion, by offending against a fundamental doctrine of our great prophet Lustrog, in the fifty–fourth Chapter of the Blundecral (which is their Alcoran). This, however, is thought to be a mere strain upon the text; for the words are these: 'that all true believers break their eggs at the convenient end.' And which is the convenient end, seems, in my humble opinion to be left to every man's conscience, or at least in the power of the chief magistrate to determine. Now, the Big–endian exiles have found so much credit in the emperor of Blefuscu's court, and so much private assistance and encouragement from their party here at home, that a bloody war has been carried on between the two empires for six–and–thirty moons, with various success; during which time we have lost forty capital ships, and a much a greater number of smaller vessels, together with thirty thousand of our best seamen and soldiers; and the damage received by the enemy is reckoned to be somewhat greater than ours. However, they have now equipped a numerous fleet, and are just preparing to make a descent upon us; and his imperial majesty, placing great confidence in your valour and strength, has commanded me to lay this account of his affairs before you."

I desired the secretary to present my humble duty to the emperor; and to let him know, "that I thought it would not become me, who was a foreigner, to interfere with parties; but I was ready, with the hazard of my life, to defend his person and state against all invaders."*

I brought myself back from the fancies in my head, to reality once again.

"Can you believe that," she was saying. "The very day she died, and those bastards decide to invade? All hell will break loose, and I'm glad she's not here to see it. She loved being deployed to the Falklands. It was one of her favourite places. And once there she'd send me photos of the wildlife she'd taken when out and about with her camera:

Killer whales, dolphins, elephant seals and sea lions. Fur seals, herons and egrets. Macaroni penguins and teal. And she always managed to put a note in the envelope telling me when she'd be home."

Docking on the sixth at 14.00. Home next day by noon.

"And they always excited me, the letters, when I received them. Photos and a written note."

And she was right.

All hell did break loose; and three days later a task force was dispatched to retake the islands at once. Returning home broken men and women to be thrown straight onto the heap.

And they were thrown onto the heap - along with the rest of the working-class community - as the Wicked Witch of the West set to work dismantling the unions and privatising state-owned business as fast as she could. Others - those in a position to do so - were only in it for the money and to make as much as they could as fast as they could.

In it for themselves and bugger the rest.

Loads of, fucking, money.

We made arrangements to attend the funeral then made our way on our own.

3

"Oh, don't go like that!" cried the poor Queen, wringing her hands in despair. "Consider what a great girl you are. Consider what a very long way you've come to-day. Consider what o'clock it is. Consider anything, only don't cry." *

Jules and Lena arrived in the middle of June 84, and we were really pleased to see them.

We'd received a letter and card at Christmas, asking if they could come visit in the summer, and stay a month or two. To which we replied, it would be nice to see them, and to come whenever they wished; and stay as long as they liked.

We'd exchanged addresses on our first meeting at David and Rosa's place at Lannion, never for a minute expecting them to visit as they said they would. We took it as the usual hot air people have a tendency to spout from time to time when they find themselves in these situations.

"Anyone here got paper and pen?" That was the usual question.

They were here now, and as both Joyce and myself were not the type to make anyone feel unwelcome - apart from her sister Janine - we made them feel at home. Or as best we could under the circumstances we now happened to find ourselves in, having both lost our jobs, thanks to Thatcher's economic policies, both of us now drawing dole.

We managed.

The prepper supplies Joyce had laid down were now coming into their own.

We picked them up from Edinburgh Airport as arranged, Neil's old car coming to the rescue again, as it always had a habit of doing whenever there was a call for wheels. Transport to get us from A to B, it was always there when I asked.

We made the journey to the cottage in quick time then slowly unpacked the bags.

Once inside, Jules was amazed his painting was on display.

"Ah, Der Führer," he said, as he entered the kitchen and saw it there hanging on the wall.

"I didn't know whether or not you'd hang it when you got home. And I said as much to Lena.

Lena, didn't I say as much to you; I wasn't convinced they'd hang it?"

"Mmm. You did," came Lena's smiling reply. "We weren't too sure about that.

And another thing. The series of paintings he completed at Lannion didn't go down well in Berlin, once we got home and showed them. We exhibited them in a gallery, situated to the rear of the house, we'd specifically set up for the purpose. It may have had to do with the manner in which they were painted - using the cock and balls not to everyone's taste - they didn't move. And to this day they languish at the back of a cupboard in the hall.

One time we get them out and show them again. What do you think Jules; maybe we sell one?"

"Should have brought them here," said Joyce, opening a bottle of wine. "We'd have hung them on a wall."

We laughed at that then we all took a seat. Made ourselves comfortable, listened to music, then they told us of the death of their cat, Flauschig …

In the midst of dinner, my mistress's favourite cat leaped into her lap. I heard a noise behind me like that of a dozen stocking–weavers at work; and turning my head, I found it proceeded from the purring of that animal, who seemed to be three times larger than an ox, as I computed by the view of her head, and one of her paws, while her mistress was feeding and stroking her. The fierceness of this creature's countenance altogether discomposed me; though I stood at the farther end of the table, above fifty feet off; and although my mistress held her fast, for fear she might give a spring, and seize me in her talons. But it happened there was no danger, for the cat took not the least notice of me when my master placed me within three yards of her. And as I have been always told, and found true by experience in my travels, that flying or discovering fear before a fierce animal, is a certain way to make it pursue or attack you, so I resolved, in this dangerous juncture, to show no manner of concern. I walked with intrepidity five or six times before the very head of the cat, and came within half a yard of her; whereupon she drew herself back, as if she were more afraid of me: I had less *apprehension concerning the dogs, whereof three or four came into the room, as it is usual in farmers' houses; one of which was a mastiff, equal in bulk to four elephants, and another a greyhound, somewhat taller than the mastiff, but not so large.**

… "We let it out at six in the morning, then heard it had been hit by a bus."

I was off on another planet, as I only caught, "… a bus."

It wasn't as if I hadn't been listening, I had. Only I hadn't been listening to what was being said. My mind off elsewhere. Off in a place of its own making, thinking of a book I had read.

The mining of words is a difficult task, and often open-cast.

I gave myself a shake then momentarily was back in the room, wishing I'd heard what he'd said. I knew I'd get the story from Joyce, later, once we were lying in bed. Tucked up tight with a sandwich and a drink, discussing the happenings of the day.

In the interim things were about to get wusrt, to make them feel at home: Currywurst to be exact … served on cardboard trays. God bless Herta Charlotte Heuwer and her culinary ingenuity. They were unaware what was about to be served, as we'd kept it from them as surprise; We were like that.

We dished it up with chips and a beer and they couldn't believe their eyes.

Berliners in Scotland dining on Currywurst, doesn't get better than that.

We first encountered the dish at a Schnellimbisse on the outskirts of Düsseldorf, on our journey to

Rheindahlen and were then given the rundown on it's history by the snack stand owner, whose mastery of the English language happened to be impeccable. We were impressed. And as soon as we knew Jules and Lena were about to visit, made up or minds to do whatever we could to serve it up. From what we'd heard and were led to believe, it was almost their national dish.

We sourced a dozen bratwurst, then I set to finding a recipe to make a beautiful curry sauce:

> 1 cup ketchup (Pudliszki's or Heinz)
> 4 tsp Madras curry powder
> 2 tsp paprika
> 2 tsp Worcester sauce
> 2 tsp honey
> 1 tsp Madras curry powder

Sprinkle with a dusting of the yellow Madras then serve with chips and beer. A veritable feast indeed for all.

Their faces when called to table that night marked with sheer delight.

4

Next morning, after a breakfast of boiled eggs, cold meat, cheese, bread and coffee, we gave over the back room in the cellar to them for art purposes, once we'd shown them where it was. And it wasn't long before they'd named it Little India, for obvious reasons, and were spending their mornings there painting and writing verse.

They grew to love it, and the storeroom they had to pass through to gain access was of particular interest, as they couldn't quite get their heads round why anyone should feel the need to build such a stock of food in the likelihood Armageddon was about to kick in. Then when we explained the situation, and the political unrest we'd been subject to as the previous Labour government crumbled under pressure from the unions and the impending doom looming over the entire nation of Scotland, under Thatcherism, they were happy enough. They understood us right away and got where we were at.

"I paint you a portrait of Thatcher," said Jules. "Another you can hang on your wall."

"That'd be nice," said Joyce, rather jokingly. "Make sure she looks like an arse."

"I will," he said, then gave a chuckle … "Even give moustache."

We all laughed, as we walked to the car. Climbed in then closed the doors.

That afternoon we took a trip out to Lochgoilhead and the surrounding area, as through conversation over breakfast it became clear our guests were not the castle and old ruins type, more inclined to stroll along a beach or take to the countryside instead.

Jules said that castles and historical ruins had always put them in mind of building sites and left them cold, and that they couldn't understand why people visited such attractions.

"Perhaps that's what we're missing," he'd continued; "The word, attraction."

It wasn't for them, he insisted. They didn't attract. They much preferred the wilds.

There was nothing better than taking in the Beauty of Great Nature, he'd said. And for that reason, they liked outdoors. A stroll along a beautiful, windswept beach or a walk in a forest where the sun filters down through the branches and treetops above.

"That's the reason we took up naturism," he said. "It makes us feel alive. At one with our fellow man and nature. In Germany we call it Freikörperkulur. A thing the UK could benefit from if the news they've been feeding us on television and the newspapers back home is anything to go by. It sounds, from what we're being told, the entire country is at each others' throats, without exception. There seems to be a proliferation of unrest sweeping the land. Only at the end of last year," he went on, "we watched police drag off women at Greenham Common as they protested against nuclear weapons being sited at the RAF base. Now it looks like things are really about to implode, what with the miner's strike and all. The Lady is not for turning. And as for the people who support her; both Lena and myself have always been of the mind that following others is a dangerous activity that can only end in disaster."

I didn't know what to say.

Joyce quipped in that Thatcher was a cunt, "and the sooner we're rid the better."

From Lochgoilhead we made our way to Inveraray and the Inverary Hotel, where we hoped to sample their gorgeous oysters and a glass of stout - though as I was named the designated driver it was cola or water for me.

"Two dozen oysters, three pints of Guinness, a coke, and Tabasco sauce. Please."

We sat by a window that overlooked the loch. Mist hanging heavy on the hills.

"The sun was shining on the sea,
    Shining with all his might:
He did his very best to make
    The billows smooth and bright -
And this was odd, because it was
    The middle of the night.

The moon was shining sulkily,
    Because she thought the sun
Had got no business to be there
    After the day was done -
"It's very rude of him," she said,
    "To come and spoil the fun."

The sea was wet as wet could be,
 The sands were dry as dry.
You could not see a cloud, because
 No cloud was in the sky:
No birds were flying overhead -
 There were no birds to fly.

The Walrus and the Carpenter
 Were walking close at hand;
They wept like anything to see
 Such quantities of sand:
If this were only cleared away,'
 They said, it would be grand!'

If seven maids with seven mops
 Swept it for half a year,
Do you suppose,' the Walrus said,
 That they could get it clear?'
I doubt it,' said the Carpenter,
 And shed a bitter tear.

O Oysters, come and walk with us!'
 The Walrus did beseech.
A pleasant walk, a pleasant talk,
 Along the briny beach:
We cannot do with more than four,
 To give a hand to each.'

The eldest Oyster looked at him,
 But never a word he said:
The eldest Oyster winked his eye,
 And shook his heavy head -

Meaning to say he did not choose
  To leave the oyster-bed.

But four young Oysters hurried up,
  All eager for the treat:
Their coats were brushed, their faces washed,
  Their shoes were clean and neat -
And this was odd, because, you know,
  They hadn't any feet.

Four other Oysters followed them,
  And yet another four;
And thick and fast they came at last,
  And more, and more, and more -
All hopping through the frothy waves,
  And scrambling to the shore.

The Walrus and the Carpenter
  Walked on a mile or so,
And then they rested on a rock
  Conveniently low:
And all the little Oysters stood
  And waited in a row.

The time has come.' the Walrus said,
  To talk of many things:
Of shoes - and ships - and sealing-wax -
  Of cabbages - and kings -
And why the sea is boiling hot -
  And whether pigs have wings.'

But wait a bit,' the Oysters cried,
  Before we have our chat;

For some of us are out of breath,
    And all of us are fat!'
No hurry!' said the Carpenter.
    They thanked him much for that.

A loaf of bread,' the Walrus said,
    Is what we chiefly need:
Pepper and vinegar besides
    Are very good indeed -
Now if you're ready, Oysters dear,
    We can begin to feed.'

But not on us!' the Oysters cried,
    Turning a little blue.
After such kindness, that would be
    A dismal thing to do!'
The night is fine,' the Walrus said.
    Do you admire the view?

It was so kind of you to come!
    And you are very nice!'
The Carpenter said nothing but
    Cut us another slice:
I wish you were not quite so deaf -
    I've had to ask you twice!'

It seems a shame,' the Walrus said,
    To play them such a trick,
After we've brought them out so far,
    And made them trot so quick!'
The Carpenter said nothing but
    The butter's spread too thick!'

*I weep for you,' the Walrus said:
  I deeply sympathize.'
With sobs and tears he sorted out
  Those of the largest size,
Holding his pocket-handkerchief
  Before his streaming eyes.*

*O Oysters,' said the Carpenter,
  You've had a pleasant run!
Shall we be trotting home again?'
  But answer came there none -
And this was scarcely odd, because
  They'd eaten every one."**

And we had. We stayed for another two hours and ordered another four dozen to be brought.

5

Then the mad-o-meter blew its top, insanity gushing from its neck.

Jellyfish swarm and shark attack. Everyman for himself.

The day had been enjoyable enough, as we'd started it off with a bowl of congee topped with chicken and peas, sliced spring onion, and a chilli oil drizzle to go.

Ha. "A chilli oil drizzle to go?" asked Joyce, as she offered the squeeze-bottle up.

Then.

We each took a turn to drench our porridge with beautiful spicy heat.

"Today we'll stay mostly in India," said Jules. Feeling to get a little artwork done. Lena to get words on a page.

"Do you think this may be possible? We feel the need to work."

"Of course," said Joyce. "Help yourselves. Use it as you see fit. You'll love the ambiance of the place. It's really got a calming effect on body and mind. You'll be able to find your muse without too much of a problem. Light a stick or two of incense. You'll find them in the bookcase drawer … And do feel free to get naked," she said … "So long as you keep it in the cellar."

"Fine … This is good," said Lena, as she pointed to the congee in her bowl with her spoon. "Very good indeed."

Once we'd tidied and swept the kitchen - Jules and Lena shipped off to India for a while - we decanted to the living room and the large sofa facing the television, ready to mong for the day.

We'd a slew of videos to watch, and with Jules and Lena having taken themselves to the cellar, we considered it time to do that and took the opportunity. And although we'd seen them often, each time we ran them and watched them again there was always scenes we'd missed.

We made a pot of tea then lifted a ten pack of Tunnock's Teacakes, covered ourselves with a patchwork quilt then settled to watch number one: The Servant; A disturbing film about class and sex with Dirk Bogarde playing lead. An insidious and insinuating servant by the name of Hugo Barrett.

This was one that disturbed us both. If only slightly.

Joyce pressed play, from her end of the couch, and we watched with legs intertwined.

Great.

Intermission we went to the kitchen, loaded up with popcorn and juice. A large bag of Jazzie's, Black Jack and Pacers. Space Dust and Rainbow Drops.

Back for the second feature of the day: Entertaining Mr Sloane.

Murder to sadism.

Homosexuality
  and everything in-between.
Nymphomania.
Bisexuality
  up on the silver screen.

Somebody Stole My Thunder,
  played
by a man named Georgie Fame,
as we readied to watch
  this adaptation
of Orton's play again.

I opened the packet of chocolate Jazzie's and started stuffing them in, and by the time I heard Jules and Lena in the kitchen - preparing an afternoon coffee for themselves - Joyce was fast asleep and the credits to Midnight Cowboy were scrolling slowly up through the screen. She'd closed her eyes midway through the previous film, and rather than disturb her by waking her up I let her lie where she was; snoring like a navvy and drivelling drool to the cushion where she rested her head.

"Joyce."

I gave her a shake and she opened her eyes; asked, "Have I been asleep?"

"Only for an hour, hour and a half; I Didn't have the heart to wake you.

Jules and Lena are up from the cellar. They're making coffee."

She threw off the quilt then got to her feet. "What did I miss?" she asked.

"Nothing much. Midnight Cowboy. I know you're not keen on that one, so I put it on while you slept. Not that often you do fall asleep, so I figured I'd fit it in.

Everybody's talkin' at me …"

She shook her head then made for the kitchen. I followed on at her back.

"How was your day?" she said to Lena. "Milk and two in mine."

"Very good," came Lena's reply. "Really quite productive. We managed to get quite a bit done each. Painting and writing verse."

"Quite a bit indeed," said Jules, handing his wife the sugar.

I reached in the cupboard for the powdered milk and a packet of McVitie's Rich Tea. Jules was a dunker, and I knew from experience he'd need two or three; and that was only for his first cup. After that he was like a madman on the rampage and there was no rectifying the situation bar taking the biscuits away, and that would have been rude. Best leave him carry on until he was stuffed and said he'd had enough. "Thanks."

By half past five we were sitting at dinner, talking, with the radio on.

Joyce had knocked up a meal of Spam fritters, Smash-mash, and baked beans, straight from our underground cache. And by the hell, I can tell you now, it all went down a treat. What in god's name was there not to like when all was said and done?

Jules mopped his plate with a slice of bread whilst Lena got up for more.

After we finished, we retired to the living room to catch the news on tv. *Flip.*

BBC1, the images flashed hard across the screen.

Jules and Lena were horrified, along with Joyce and myself. This was Britain for god's sake. Britain. It didn't happen here. Things like this happened other places. They didn't happen here. Joyce had called it on PM Thatcher and hit the nail on the head. "A mad-ass bitch," she'd said at the time and now she was showing her hand. She'd beat the striking miners to submission, then flood the mines. Kill off the industry once and for all, with the truncheon and battle charge.

Confrontation had happened before. This was somewhat different. Downright vicious thuggery it was, reported in the usual biased way.

And as I took it all in from the living room sofa, madrigals played in my head - incessant. The Battle of Orgreave, police brutality, baton charges and dogs.

Lena looked to Jules.

"Alarmingly reminiscent of the Sturmabteilung in our own country, prior der Krieg," she said. "Don't you think?"

Jules was fixed to the tv screen as strikers queued at ROCK ON TOMMY and mounted forces attacked. Baton charges from atop their steeds, hitting as hard as they could. Orders.

No one was turning back miner's this day. Welcomed with open arms. Come in.

Jules turned to Joyce and told her that Thatcher was Hitler in a skirt; to him at any rate.

"You have nothing but trouble from her," he said. "Act before it's too late. We have always been of the frame of mind that people who follow others are gullible and have always looked on that type of behaviour as dangerous. I hear she's stealing the National Front vote; this you need to watch."

Agendas and running sheets weren't for them. They could think for themselves.

I pulled the plug and shot the haunted-fish-tank back to black.

The question to be debated was, "whether the Yahoos should be exterminated from the face of the earth?" One of the members for the affirmative offered several arguments of great strength and weight, alleging, "that as the Yahoos were the most filthy, noisome, and deformed animals which nature ever produced, so they were the most restive and indocible, mischievous and malicious; they would privately suck the teats of the Houyhnhnms' cows, kill and devour their cats, trample down their oats and grass, if they were not continually watched, and commit a thousand other extravagancies." He took notice of a general tradition, "that Yahoos had not been always in their country; but that many ages ago, two of these brutes appeared together upon a mountain; whether produced by the heat of the sun upon corrupted mud and slime, or from the ooze and froth of the sea, was never known; that these Yahoos engendered, and their brood, in a short time, grew so numerous as to overrun and infest the whole nation; that the Houyhnhnms, to get rid of this evil, made a general hunting, and at last *enclosed the whole herd; and destroying the elder, every Houyhnhnm kept two young ones in a kennel, and brought them to such a degree of tameness, as an animal, so savage by nature, can be capable of acquiring, using them for draught and carriage; that there seemed to be much truth in this tradition, and that those creatures could not be yinhniamshy (or aborigines of the land), because of the violent hatred the Houyhnhnms, as well as all other animals, bore them, which, although their evil disposition sufficiently deserved, could never have arrived at so high a degree if they had been aborigines, or else they would have long since been rooted out; that the inhabitants, taking a fancy to use the service of the Yahoos, had, very imprudently, neglected to cultivate the breed of asses, which are a comely animal, easily kept, more tame and orderly, without any offensive smell, strong enough for labour, although they yield to the other in agility of body, and if their braying be no agreeable sound, it is far preferable to the horrible howlings of the Yahoos."**

Jules and Lena were gone by the end of July, and as promised they left us a sample of their work in the cellar: A portrait of Thatcher - looking like an arse as requested by Joyce, that on closer inspection did look as if he had used his arse for the outline of her head before rendering the rest of her features by using various other of his body parts - and a poem by Lena for us both:

Feast

Beauty of Great Nature devour our cities, *Feast*
on our runways and planes. *Feast.*

Feast on our stations that stand by the track
their metal signs boasting their names. *Feast.*

Swallow our churches, chapels and mosques
gorge on our concrete and shame. *Feast.*

Chow down whatever you find as man-made
gobble our shackles and chains. *Feast.*

Feast as you will on Victorian promenades
crumble the Benben stones. *Feast.*

Crunch through our graveyards silent and dark
push up our ancestor's bones. *Feast.*

Gulp up our motorways narrow and straight
suck the perimeter zones. *Feast.*

Feast as you will with incessant belligerence
settle yourself on that throne. *Feast.*

We framed them then hung them in the kitchen along side the portrait of Der Führer. And like Der Führer, those in opposition to what Thatcher and her government represented - though in this case in opposition to British rule in whatever guise it was being shoved down their throats - tried to blow her up. Unfortunately, much akin the failed attempt by

Claus von Stauffenbeg to rid his country of Hitler, the IRA did likewise. Their Bomb at the Grand Hotel, Brighton, failing to carry her off.

It was a good attempt, though with a long-delay time bomb primed to go off at two fifty-four in the morning when it was hoped that Thatcher and her cabinet, who had turned up en masse for the Conservative Party conference and were staying for the duration would be tucked-up safely in bed. And they were. The only problem being that when the bomb exploded it killed five and Thatcher was left unscathed; A five-ton chimney stack crashing down through numerous floors into the basement below. Ripping a hole in the hotel's façade like a ladder being ripped in nylon.

Lucky for her she hadn't been on the pan evacuating her bowel at the time. For the thing crashed through her suite's bathroom, narrowly missing her living and bedroom where it was later confirmed she'd been working on her next days conference speech.

Thirty-four people were injured in the attack. Some permanently disabled.

Still, left to ride another day, the lady was not for turning.

6

Eleven and a half month after it started the miner's strike ended in victory for Thatcher and the Tory government, and by the end of the year I was working in a clothing warehouse, driving a fork-truck and generally man-handling goods into the back of forty-foot trailers ready to be shipped nationwide.

Joyce was working, three days a week, in the village bakery, a mile and a half away, and walked the distance each day, returning with cakes and pies; the occasional loaf of freshly baked bread, pancakes and tattie scones. Now we were starting to feed ourselves, albeit most of it stodge.

In the 1980s health consciousness wasn't quite a thing yet.

And it was then I got my licence back and we bought a second-hand motorcycle with sidecar. A 1960 Matchless 650cc, with a black and red Watsonian, mounted on the left-hand side. *Brrrmm.*

This gave us the freedom to travel, that up until then we lacked; It always being the case that whenever we did need transport, we always relied on the kindness of Neil to furnish a set of wheels. Which he always did readily, no questions asked. This was different. These wheels were ours. The freedom to travel wherever we liked changed the game. And the first weekend that came with free time we loaded up and headed for the hills.

The Silver Sands of Morar, where we had the time of our lives.

We set off on the Friday about five and took the scenic route up through the A82 towards Oban - passed The Green Welly at Tyndrum where we called in for toilet and tea; stretched the legs for twenty minutes then climbed aboard once again.

We arrived at our final destination coming up for half past ten. Then throwing our tent up down on the sand, climbed in our sleeping bags. No need to report to reception here, this was what we called wild camping. The way both Joyce and myself preferred it and liked to spend our time.

We'd brought a small radio along, and under the light, we'd hung overhead, we tuned it to Radio 1.

Ten minutes later we were both asleep, snoring like pigs in a sty.

The following morning I was up at five and switched the radio off; took a stroll on the beach. I determined to leave Joyce asleep rather than disturb her, when in all probability she was already awake in her head somewhere, living her life in a dream: Taking it easy in a foreign city, watching the people go by. Smoking a gold tipped Sobranie Black Russian, sitting by a café in a square.

"Una taza de café más, por favor. Y una rebanada de tarta San Marcos."

Then almost as quick she'd be sitting with her sister, who wasn't her sister but her cousin.

Standing in a bar in New York city with Jagger and David Jones.

I picked up driftwood and bits and pieces washed ashore by the tide. Dropped them as soon as I'd inspected what they were, walked along to the next. I played on a rope-swing for ten to fifteen minutes, then made my way back to the tent, where I unpacked the Colman from its carry-case and sparked the thing to life. Filled a pot from a bottle of water then proceeded to make us both coffee. I felt like a cup after my walk and had it in my mind that as soon as Joyce woke, she'd feel the same. It was now six thirty and I knew by seven she'd open her eyes. Then right on cue at six fifty-five she opened said peepers and smiled.

"Morning," she said, as she sat herself up, rubbing her head in her hands. "What time is it?"

"Five to seven," I said, as I spooned a measure of coffee in a cup. "Coffee?"

"That'd be great. What's it like outside?"

She knew instinctively I'd been up early and had gone for a walk. She didn't need to enquire as she already knew that on the first morning of our arrival, be it wherever, I'd always be up as early as I could and take myself for a walk. It was a ritual, and if the destination was one we'd frequented frequently the routine would still be the same: Up early, out for a walk, back for coffee or tea - usually coffee unless I had brought loose-leaf Assam along. Which on this trip I had optioned against.

"Beautiful," I said. "Not a cloud in the sky. And if my instinct tells me anything, it'll be fine all day."

I handed her the coffee, and she lit a cigarette, handed it over to me.

"Thanks."

She lit another for herself, inhaled, then exhaled the smoke through her nose.

"Find anything?"

"Nothing to speak of. The usual assortment of trash and driftwood you usually find. Plastic bottles and empty crisp bags. Then I found cuttlefish bones. It took time to figure out what they were. They were lying next to a rubber duck and an old trainer, and at first, I surmised it was pumice. Then my brain took a different tack and I started to think it was ambergris. That was wishful thinking. Cuttlefish bones in the end."

She laughed then took a sip of her coffee.

"What we got planned for today?"

"I'd an idea we'd take a ride to Mallaig and catch a bite to eat in the Mission Café, then pick up food and drink."

We'd brought a disposable BBQ along, and as the weather looked like staying fine all day as forecast, we were looking forward to a cook-up on the beach.

We finished our coffee then took a stroll along the shoreline with its beautiful scenery and views across The Sound of Sleat, out to the Isle of Skye.

We were only killing time before the six minute drive to Mallaig, as the walk would set us up for breakfast; give us a bit of an appetite to stuff in bacon and eggs.

Back at the tent we killed another hour then left at ten. And as we'd parked in a small carpark, with an old toilet block at the far end, about two or three hundred yards from where we'd set up camp, we made up our mind to go: As having used the dunes to the rear of our tent since arriving last night and this morning, civilization beckoned. Best give it a go, to see what it was like. It soon became clear we shouldn't have bothered. Neither of us got to go.

The place was a midden. A pure dunghill with shit overflowing the bombed-out pans, graffiti on the walls, a profusion of litter, and a stench that could knock you out. Bring you to your knees if you were fool enough to spend any time in the place.

We both came out in unison, laughed then uttered, "Fuck."

We'd hold it till we got to the Mission then do our business there. Wash our hands then order breakfast, sit down and savour our meal.

And before we knew it, we were. Sausage bacon and eggs. Two rounds of toast, butter and jam. Tea and a roll-up each. Bliss.

"You know," I said, finishing off a crust. "They used to call this place Chinatown; Mallaig I mean," to clarify, in case she was thinking the Mission.

"How come? Was it full of Chinkies? Funny place for them to come to. It's a touch out of the way."

Shit, I could have slapped her there and then; I managed to bite my lip. Telling her off in the past for her use of derogatory terms had no effect. Maybe keeping my mouth shut would elicit the opposite. I doubted it very much. I didn't think it to be the case for a minute. She was too far gone for that. And I didn't hold out that one day she'd suddenly modify her vocabulary, where people's ethnicities were involved. That was a bit of a long shot.

"No." I said, in reply to her question. "Not because they were here. There weren't any Chinese here; well, not that I'm aware of anyway. It was because that in one part of town where they smoked herring the accommodation constructed for migrant worker was less that affluent by anybody's standard. They were nothing more than wooden huts. Jerry-built you'd term them. Not salubrious by any mean."

"So where did the people come from," she asked, "if they didn't come from China?"

"Itinerant workers and groups of herring girls." I said. "All over, really. The Lowlands and Islands, and wherever the hell people were struggling to find employment."

This satisfied her curiosity, though she did say, "No Chinese?"

We made ourselves another roll-up then took a walk to the harbour.

We were back at the Sands by half twelve, loaded with sausage, burgers and wine, and were pleased to see, in the time we were gone, another couple had set up camp a short distance along the shore from us, and were already making themselves comfortable in portable, folding, camping chairs - cup holder in each of the right-hand arm rests, a windbreak and striped beach parasol.

From what I could discern, from the distance I was at, they looked to be drinking K. And as that was the only can with a big red K on the side of it I knew, I took it that that's what it was.

We waved our hellos as we bent to the tent, dropped off our helmets and bags. Opened a bottle of wine we had bought, kicked off our boots and shoes.

"Right, first things first," I said to Joyce. "Let's get ourselves in the sun. Grab the cups, and the radio there. I've got the wine and cards."

I lifted the folding portable stools, and we made our way to the sun. Perfect.

In no time at all the tin cups we'd brought were full of red wine and cheer.

The afternoon passed in glorious sunshine, much as we expected it would, and we spent the time playing cards and listening to the radio, lying on the sand using our stools more as armrests than implements you sat on. We played rummy and switch, and Joyce filled me in on the shenanigans taking place in the bakery.

"He's under the illusion nobody knows. That's the impression I get."

She was on about the owner, said his name was Bob. Said he was a bit of a sleaze-ball.

"I didn't notice at first, being a newbie. I wasn't looking for it. You're keeping your head down trying to make a good impression till you settle in. Mavis Ray told me, and then she said, I should watch out for his wandering hands."

That was a laugh, because if his hands happened to wander anywhere near Joyce, he was likely to get a broken nose for his trouble.

"He's married with kids. The worse type. They're all alike. A bit of money in the bank and they think they're it. Think they've the right to put it about, and don't give a fuck about their wife, or their kids. The bastard would have to try it once and I'd give him fucking pies."

We lit the barbeque at four o'clock and by six we were sitting with our neighbours.

You know how these things go: the chat starts slowly, as it has a habit of doing in such situations, then inevitably builds to a crescendo where the full orchestra takes over and develops into a free-for-all, everyone talking over one another and bursting into song for no other reason than the alcohol's kicked in and the inhibitions have flown out the window along with reserve and dignity. The four of us now pissing behind their tent rather than walk the two hundred yards to the woods above the dunes. And as the chill kicked in about eight - along with hordes of midges - we lit a fire from wood we'd collected earlier.

"You're everywhere and nowhere, baby
That's where you're at
Going down a bumpy hillside
In your hippy hat."

Mick was prolific, I'll say that for him, but he couldn't finish a song.

"That's his trouble," said Ann-Marie, "the finish. I'm still waiting on him finishing the conservatory."

The four of us laughed at this assessment. Mick merely carried on.

"I used to be such a sweet, sweet thing

'Til they got a hold of me ..."

Random.

   I don't know where the hell he got them; suspect he pulled them from a bag.

By quarter to twelve, Joyce was pointing out stars in the sky. An hour later, we were back in our bags, listening to Father Andy.

7

Time drags its heels when your locked in employment that's slowly destroying your soul. And believe me, I knew. I knew all too well the sucking of blood that took place when you signed your life away to go work for the man.

You became a non-person, the number assigned at birth - YX 95 whatever it may be - your only means of identification, reduced to letters and numbers.

And these days, what with the defeat of the National Union of Mineworkers, and the Tories allowing countless thousands the right to buy their council properties, at vastly reduce rates, any idea of taking the fight to them through industrial action was all but confined to the past.

Now you were stuck to the Grind Machine, whether you liked it or not.

"You are old, Father William," the young man said,
 "And your hair has become very white;
And yet you incessantly stand on your head -
 Do you think, at your age, it is right?"

"In my youth," Father William replied to his son,
 "I feared it might injure the brain;
But, now that I'm perfectly sure I have none,
 Why, I do it again and again."

"You are old," said the youth, "as I mentioned before,
　And have grown most uncommonly fat;
Yet you turned a back-somersault in at the door -
　Pray, what is the reason of that?"

"In my youth," said the sage, as he shook his grey locks,
　"I kept all my limbs very supple
By the use of this ointment—one shilling the box -
　Allow me to sell you a couple?"

"You are old," said the youth, "and your jaws are too weak
　For anything tougher than suet;
Yet you finished the goose, with the bones and the beak -
　Pray, how did you manage to do it?"

"In my youth," said his father, "I took to the law,
　And argued each case with my wife;
And the muscular strength, which it gave to my jaw,
　Has lasted the rest of my life."

"You are old," said the youth, "one would hardly suppose
　That your eye was as steady as ever;
Yet you balanced an eel on the end of your nose -
　What made you so awfully clever?"

"I have answered three questions, and that is enough,"

Said his father; "don't give yourself airs!
Do you think I can listen all day to such stuff?
  Be off, or I'll kick you down stairs!"*

And still the madness prevailed, as The Bitch embarked on a privatization programme, selling off swathes of nationalized companies to a select bunch of cronies, without so much as a by your leave. She didn't need permission.

"What'll be next, that's what I'd like to know?" said Joyce. "If she can sell off the likes of British Aerospace and Rolls-Royce, anything's up for grabs. It's the old story; the rich get richer and the likes of us struggle along in a hand-to-mouth existence, barely managing to survive. It's madness. And since this lot took over it's accelerating exponentially. It's like riding a roller coaster out of control, heading straight for hell."

"You forgot to mention British Airways, they were snapped up as well."

I was of the same frame of mind as Joyce when it came to privatization.

"Mark my words," I said. "When the time's right, British Steel and the electricity companies will be next. And she won't be happy at that. She's always been for the rich and we know that. Why else would she have abolished exchange controls and cut the top rate of income tax. It wasn't for the likes of us. She's turned the City into a meritocracy and that should tell you everything you need to know about The Bitch. That and the massive increase in banker's wages.

In forty years time the economy will be broken. People will be struggling to put food on their tables. Choosing between heat or eat."

Joyce looked up from the paper she was reading; folded it, then put it down.

"See, prepping's not such a bad idea after all. Is it?" she said.

I had to admit I was changing my mind and slowly coming round to the scheme. In the past I hadn't been out-and-out against it. I was merely of the impression the people involved in the whole prepping business were a bunch of cranks and fanatics. The sort of right-wing arseholes Joyce had always, vehemently, decried in private and public. These days, with the passing of time, and all that was going wrong with the country, my views had hardened a ways. And the threat I envisioned was not one of ultra right-wing thugs marching to bring down the government. It was the actual government itself. These crazy arseholes were out to destroy the country from within. And were doing a damn good job.

Joyce got up and filled the kettle, placed the thing on the hob.

"Coffee?"

She turned and looked at herself in the mirror, lifted a finger to her nose.

"Look," she said. "A spot. Right there on the end of my nose. A spot that's coming up."

I told her to leave the thing alone and it'd go away.

"Squeezing it will only make it worse," I told her. "Leave the thing alone. No one's going to notice. Hardly see the thing."

The doorbell rang as the kettle boiled. I went to see who it was."

Well.

You can imagine the shock on my face, when I opened it and was confronted by Janine, standing there with a case, in the rain, soaked to skin and bone.

I was about to ask her what she wanted - as Joyce had made it perfectly clear, at their last meeting, under no circumstances was she to return - then decided against it when my better judgement came into play. After all, she wasn't my sister, and going by the look on her face, standing there in the pissing rain, I figured it must be important.

I lifted her case then told her, "Come in; walked along the hall to the kitchen.

Joyce's face was a picture when we entered, and it struck me she might explode.

"I told you not to come back?" she said. "Are you thick or did you not understand?"

She looked at me as if to say, "Why did you let her in?"

I shrugged my shoulders, lifted my leathers, helmet, then made for the door.

Forty minutes later I was driving along the front at South Queensferry, having made up my mind there and then, as soon as Joyce drew me the look she had, to bugger off out of it.

I parked-up and walked along the front to The Hawes Inn where I had a mind to grab myself a bite to eat and put as much distance between the sisters and myself as I could.

Then, once I'd ordered my meal and it came, that's exactly what I did. Took myself completely out of the equation, and turned my imagination to Robert Louis Stevenson, and Kidnapped.

I knew from reading, in the past, that it was here in The Hawes he'd started writing the work, and I could easily envisage him sitting at a window seat before retiring to his bedroom where he concocted the idea, and where the kidnapping of the books hero, David Balfour, was arranged.

And I was also aware it was Fidra, a small rocky outcrop, off the coast of North Berwick, on the Firth, that he'd visited as a child with is father, that was the inspiration for the map for Treasure Island.

It was one of those places writers were drawn, and as far as I could recall, The Inn is also mentioned in Stevenson's, Memories and Portraits, then once again in Sir Walter Scott's, Antiquary; although the less said about him the better.

I imagined Stevenson sitting at the window watching the construction of the bridge in awe, having shown no aptitude at university for engineering himself - the family profession of lighthouse design in no way was tugging at his strings - over a glass of wine.

I finished my lunch then sat an hour, forming a picture in my head.

I drank two coffees and a glass of water, then walked slowly back to the bike. Time to make the return journey and find out what was happening. Get to the bottom of why Janine had turned up out of the blue the way she had. Especially when she'd been told by Joyce, not to come back after their last confrontation.

I didn't return the way I'd come. I took the long way round.

I made my way over the road bridge with a mind to drive to Culross, down passed the palace, then out along the road toward the Kincardine bridge, Skinflats, Polmont then home.

I reckoned the three hours I'd have been gone, once I returned, would have been enough time for the pair of them to sort out whatever it was that required sorting out, and either be embracing one another or be further apart than ever they were. Joyce having banished her for good.

I parked the bike then draped it in its cover, removed my helmet and boots.

Inside, Joyce was sitting on her own in the kitchen drinking a mug of tea.

"Is she gone?" I asked, as I couldn't see her case, so presumed she had.

"No, she's in the spare room," she said, rather matter-of-factly. "She'll be staying a while."

You could have dropped me with a flower when I heard this; Staying? Seriously. What the hell could have taken place within three hours that could possibly have resulted in a decision such as this? Bribery of a sort I couldn't imagine? It had to be good.

"Staying?" I said, when I caught my breath, with more than a touch of surprise. "What brought this about then," I asked, "someone been drinking the water?"

"Warren's been messing again, and she can't forgive him. She said she's had enough."

"And who is he messing with," I asked, "that's made her act like this? Didn't seem to bother her before?"

"Well," said Joyce. "According to her there's a new family moved in next door with an eighteen-year-old daughter, and it only took him three weeks to get her into bed. She'd have been none the wiser if she hadn't arrived home from work unexpectedly and caught them at it on the living room sofa. That," she said, "was the last straw."

"Age of majority," I said to myself. The words came out real loud.

"Be that as it may," said Joyce, in return. "He's always been a fucking dick."

"Why is she staying here? Why not with mum or Ron? More to the point; Why did you let her stay, after everything she's said about you? You know she's a bitch and can't keep her mouth shut for more than a minute at a time. Besides, she's told you on more than one occasion this place freaks her out, so why the hell would she stay. If a place freaked me out that much, I wouldn't spend a night, never mind arrive with a suitcase full of clothes and move in. The mind boggles, doesn't it, Joyce. Heigh-ho, she's your sister."

"And that's exactly it. She's my sister. And I couldn't for the life of me have her staying in a seedy hotel room on the edge of a dead-end town. Now, could I? And as for mum or uncle Ron, completely out of the question. What they don't know won't hurt them, so best keep this to ourselves.

She left without a penny, so till she gets herself sorted and finds a place to stay, we'll have to put up with her."

She stood then looked in the mirror again; burst the spot on her nose.

8

And still she came on like a runaway train.

Who could forget the attack posters that raised their ugly heads during the 87 campaign. Neither Joyce nor myself. We felt sickened by them. Especially: IS THIS LABOUR'S IDEA OF A COMPREHENSIVE EDUCATION? What the hell was that about, could anyone tell us?

"Have you seen this in the paper?" said Joyce, a touch of rage in her voice. "Closer to a fascist state with each passing day."

"What is it?" I said. Intrigued to see what the Tories were up to now."

"This here Section 28 nonsense. It's as bad as the Buggery Act, and that was passed in the 16th century. Who the hell do the Tories think they are? As if gay men don't have enough to contend with, what with HIV/AIDS. Look at this poster in the paper. Disgraceful."

She slid the paper across the table, open at the offending page. A large poster, on a hoarding on a corner, screamed homophobic rage. I looked at it twice to see what it said on each individual book: Young gay & proud. Police: Out of School! The playbook for kids about sex.

God.

The country was getting nuttier by the day with this woman in charge. And this was by no means a sexist or misogynistic statement, merely an observation. Who in their correct mind would pass such a draconian law that prohibits local authorities from intentionally promoting homosexuality, or promoting the teaching in schools of the acceptability of it as a pretended family relationship, and feel proud having done so?

These were dangerous times my friend. Very dangerous indeed.

They had to have been. For if a party can distribute posters such as the above, and the likes of the Monday Club's Jill Knight could say, without fear of recrimination, that The Milkman's on his Way was being taught to children as young as five in schools, then something was seriously amiss.

The act was enabled in 88.

Me thinks you protest too much.

As I ought to have understood human nature much better than I supposed it possible for my master to do, so it was easy to apply the character he gave of the Yahoos to myself and my countrymen; and I believed I could yet make further discoveries, from my own observation. I therefore often begged his honour to let me go among the herds of Yahoos in the neighbourhood; to which he always very graciously consented, being perfectly convinced that the hatred I bore these brutes would never suffer me to be corrupted by them; and his honour ordered one of his servants, a strong sorrel nag, very honest and good–natured, to be my guard; without whose protection I durst not undertake such adventures. For I have already told the reader how *much I was pestered by these odious animals, upon my first arrival; and I afterwards failed very narrowly, three or four times, of falling into their clutches, when I happened to stray at any distance without my hanger. And I have reason to believe they had some imagination that I was of their own species, which I often assisted myself by stripping up my sleeves, and showing my naked arms and breasts in their sight, when my protector was with me. At which times they would approach as near as they durst, and imitate my actions after the manner of monkeys, but ever with great signs of hatred; as a tame jackdaw with cap and stockings is always persecuted by the wild ones, when he happens to be got among them.**

Next morning when I got up Janine's words were still ringing in my ears: Poor Joyce. Self-centred. Working in a dead-end job. And as I buttered toast, before applying a thick layer of Marmite, I considered making our own. What would have been the point in that? Only pettiness. Although what would serve my purpose in the long run, I mused, would be to foster the notion there was supernatural phenomena taking place in the cellar and kitchen in the guise of a ghost, most likely Walter or the previous owner, both unable to leave. Trapped in a parallel universe, wailing and rattling pipes.

   I'd tell her we'd tried to set them free, with little success.

   I'd work on this as soon as she got up, showered and was ready to eat.

   I didn't have to wait long.

"Janine, I meant to ask. Did Joyce tell you about the spectre in the cellar? It could be Walter. We don't know. It's definitely a ghost of sorts."

I felt Joyce's eyes burn a hole in the back of my head as she stood drinking tea by the sink.

I could live with that.

It was Janine I was watching. And as I did so the colour drained rapidly from her face. It was a picture. I knew she'd flush as soon as I mentioned we may have a ghost upstairs.

"Comes to life at night in the cellar." A Beautiful oxymoron.

"Ellis," said Joyce. "What the hell did you have to tell her that for? She's enough on her plate? You know she's stressed as it is, and the doctor has signed her off work. I don't know what it is Ellis. Sometimes you don't engage that brain of yours before you open your mouth. Sometimes I think you're an eejit."

Janine got up and went to her room. Joyce sat down at the table.

"What did you tell her that for?" she said. "You know what she's like. This place freaks her out as it is, and then you tell her that. Ghosts? Where the hell did that come from … outer fucking space? Honestly Ellis, sometimes I wish you'd shut it."

At this point I suspected I'd hit a nerve that was already pretty raw.

"Why don't you fuck off to Ken's for an hour. I need to sort this out."

I was back in my leathers within ten minutes and glad to be out of the place.

When I returned things had sorted themselves out and I wished to hell I hadn't mentioned ghosts. I was only trying to help, and I surmised from the look on Janine's face she wasn't happy and was waiting for an apology before she was likely to speak. Fuck her: That's what I was thinking; not what I did. I buckled and offered up peace.

"Sorry about this morning," I said. Trying as hard as I could to make it sound sincere in the hope she'd accept what I had to say and that would be the end of it. Move along and get along. Everybody happy.

And she seemed to. And before long we were chatting away as if nothing out of the ordinary had taken place and I hadn't ruffled her feathers to begin with. Rubbed her up the wrong way then pissed her off.

You couldn't tell with Janine. When you suspected her character was changing, she'd revert to Janine of old. A torn faced, carnaptious bitch. Crabbit as hell to boot. I made up my mind, for Joyce's sake, to try and toe the line.

"Tea?"

In the end we didn't have to put up with her that long, as in the great scheme of things nine month isn't any time at all.

We considered she may have given in, like she'd done on previous occasions, and gone back to him all apologetic and sorry for acting the way she had. Walking out and calling him a cunt, without hearing his side of things.

Used to be she'd believe whatever he told her, wrapped around his finger the way she was. What changed? Conversations with Joyce? Who knows. This time she definitely dug in her heels and filed for a 'quickie' divorce. Split what they had, 50/50 down the middle, then bought herself a small flat. Changed days from the 'mansion on the hill.' And oh, how the mighty have fallen.

There you have it. In the end she stuck to her guns, and all credit to her. I never, in my wildest dreams, contemplated a split between them never mind out-and-out divorce. Usually, it's a beheading when it comes to royalty. Fortunately those days are over, and we've moved on a ways. The official headsman's position long relinquished to a judge in a robe and wig.

Lucky for her, that's all I can say. Or Warren may have had her for the chop.

Chop.

Now she was gone I reflected on the time they were forced to spend together.

Sisterly love? I didn't go that far. That was nothing but a nonsense.

I wouldn't even have gone as far as to say the time they did spend together had brought them, in any way, closer. The only conclusion I did manage to draw from the situation was that when the chips were down and either of them was in trouble then the other, inevitably, stepped to the plate. Blood is always thicker than water after all.

They'd soon be back to themselves.

9

The sharp, ear-piercing screech of a siren forces me to jump from bed.

There was a table set out under a tree in front of the house, and the March Hare and the Hatter were having tea at it: a Dormouse was sitting between them, fast asleep, and the other two were using it as a cushion, resting their elbows on it, and talking over its head. "Very uncomfortable for the Dormouse," thought Alice; "only, as it's asleep, I suppose it doesn't mind."

The table was a large one, but the three were all crowded together at one corner of it: "No room! No room!" they cried out when they saw Alice coming. "There's plenty of room!" said Alice indignantly, and she sat down in a large arm-chair at one end of the table.

"Have some wine," the March Hare said in an encouraging tone.

Alice looked all round the table, but there was nothing on it but tea. "I don't see any wine," she remarked.

"There isn't any," said the March Hare.

"Then it wasn't very civil of you to offer it," said Alice angrily.

"It wasn't very civil of you to sit down without being invited," said the March Hare.

"I didn't know it was your table," said Alice; "it's laid for a great many more than three."

"Your hair wants cutting," said the Hatter. He had been looking at Alice for some time with great curiosity, and this was his first speech.

"You should learn not to make personal remarks," Alice said with some severity; "it's very rude."

The Hatter opened his eyes very wide on hearing this; but all he said was, "Why is a raven like a writing-desk?"

"Come, we shall have some fun now!" thought Alice. "I'm glad they've begun asking riddles. - I believe I can guess that," she added aloud.

"Do you mean that you think you can find out the answer to it?" said the March Hare.

"Exactly so," said Alice.

"Then you should say what you mean," the March Hare went on.

"I do," Alice hastily replied; "at least - at least I mean what I say - that's the same thing, you know."

"Not the same thing a bit!" said the Hatter. "You might just as well say that 'I see what I eat' is the same thing as 'I eat what I see'!"

"You might just as well say," added the March Hare, "that 'I like what I get' is the same thing as 'I get what I like'!"

"You might just as well say," added the Dormouse, who seemed to be talking in his sleep, "that 'I breathe when I sleep' is the same thing as 'I sleep when I breathe'!"

"It is the same thing with you," said the Hatter, and here the conversation dropped, and the party *sat silent for a minute, while Alice thought over all she could remember about ravens and writing-desks, which wasn't much.*

The Hatter was the first to break the silence. "What day of the month is it?" he said, turning to Alice: he had taken his watch out of his pocket, and was looking at it uneasily, shaking it every now and then, and holding it to his ear.

Alice considered a little, and then said "The fourth."

"Two days wrong!" sighed the Hatter. "I told you butter wouldn't suit the works!" he added looking angrily at the March Hare.

"It was the best butter," the March Hare meekly replied.

"Yes, but some crumbs must have got in as well," the Hatter grumbled: "you shouldn't have put it in with the bread-knife."

The March Hare took the watch and looked at it gloomily: then he dipped it into his cup of tea, and looked at it again: but he could think of nothing better to say than his first remark, "It was the best butter, you know."

Alice had been looking over his shoulder with some curiosity. "What a funny watch!" she remarked. "It tells the day of the month, and doesn't tell what o'clock it is!"

"Why should it?" muttered the Hatter. "Does your watch tell you what year it is?"

"Of course not," Alice replied very readily: "but that's because it stays the same year for such a long time together."

"Which is just the case with mine," said the Hatter.

Alice felt dreadfully puzzled. The Hatter's remark seemed to have no sort of meaning in it, and yet it was certainly English. "I don't quite understand you," she said, as politely as she could.

"The Dormouse is asleep again," said the Hatter, and he poured a little hot tea upon its nose.

The Dormouse shook its head impatiently, and said, without opening its eyes, "Of course, of course; just what I was going to remark myself."

"Have you guessed the riddle yet?" the Hatter said, turning to Alice again.

"No, I give it up," Alice replied: "what's the answer?"

"I haven't the slightest idea," said the Hatter.

"Nor I," said the March Hare.

Alice sighed wearily. "I think you might do something better with the time," she said, "than waste it in asking riddles that have no answers."

"If you knew Time as well as I do," said the Hatter, "you wouldn't talk about wasting it. It's *him.*"

"I don't know what you mean," said Alice.

"Of course you don't!" the Hatter said, tossing his head contemptuously. "I dare say you never even spoke to Time!"

"Perhaps not," Alice cautiously replied: "but I know I have to beat time when I learn music."

"Ah! that accounts for it," said the Hatter. "He won't stand beating. Now, if you only kept on good terms with him, he'd do almost anything you liked with the clock. For instance, suppose it were nine *o'clock in the morning, just time to begin lessons: you'd only have to whisper a hint to Time, and round goes the clock in a twinkling! Half-past one, time for dinner!"*

("I only wish it was," the March Hare said to itself in a whisper.)

"That would be grand, certainly," said Alice thoughtfully: "but then - I shouldn't be hungry for it, you know."

"Not at first, perhaps," said the Hatter: "but you could keep it to half-past one as long as you liked."

"Is that the way you manage?" Alice asked.

The Hatter shook his head mournfully. "Not I!" he replied. "We quarrelled last March - just before he went mad, you know -" (pointing with his tea spoon at the March Hare,) "- it was at the great concert given by the Queen of Hearts, and I had to sing

*'Twinkle, twinkle, little bat!
How I wonder what you're at!'*

You know the song, perhaps?"

"I've heard something like it," said Alice.

"It goes on, you know," the Hatter continued, "in this way: -

*'Up above the world you fly,
Like a tea-tray in the sky.
Twinkle, twinkle -'"*

Here the Dormouse shook itself, and began singing in its sleep "Twinkle, twinkle, twinkle,

twinkle -" and went on so long that they had to pinch it to make it stop.

"Well, I'd hardly finished the first verse," said the Hatter, "when the Queen jumped up and bawled out, 'He's murdering the time! Off with his head!'"

"How dreadfully savage!" exclaimed Alice.

"And ever since that," the Hatter went on in a mournful tone, "he won't do a thing I ask! It's always six o'clock now."

A bright idea came into Alice's head. "Is that the reason so many tea-things are put out here?" she asked.

"Yes, that's it," said the Hatter with a sigh: "it's always tea-time, and we've no time to wash the things between whiles."

"Then you keep moving round, I suppose?" said Alice.

"Exactly so," said the Hatter: "as the things get used up."

"But what happens when you come to the beginning again?" Alice ventured to ask.

"Suppose we change the subject," the March Hare interrupted, yawning. "I'm getting tired of this. I vote the young lady tells us a story."

"I'm afraid I don't know one," said Alice, rather alarmed at the proposal.

"Then the Dormouse shall!" they both cried. "Wake up, Dormouse!" And they pinched it on both sides at once.

The Dormouse slowly opened his eyes. "I wasn't asleep," he said in a hoarse, feeble voice: "I heard every word you fellows were saying."

"Tell us a story!" said the March Hare.

"Yes, please do!" pleaded Alice.

"And be quick about it," added the Hatter, "or you'll be asleep again before it's done."

"Once upon a time there were three little sisters," the Dormouse began in a great hurry; "and their names were Elsie, Lacie, and Tillie; and they lived at the bottom of a well -"

"What did they live on?" said Alice, who always took a great interest in questions of eating and drinking.

"They lived on treacle," said the Dormouse, after thinking a minute or two.

"They couldn't have done that, you know," Alice gently remarked; "they'd have been ill."

"So they were," said the Dormouse; "very ill."

Alice tried to fancy to herself what such an extraordinary ways of living would be like, but it puzzled her too much, so she went on: "But why did they live at the bottom of a well?"

"Take some more tea," the March Hare said to Alice, very earnestly.

"I've had nothing yet," Alice replied in an offended tone, "so I can't take more."

"You mean you can't take less," said the Hatter: "it's very easy to take more than nothing."

"Nobody asked your opinion," said Alice.

"Who's making personal remarks now?" the Hatter asked triumphantly.

Alice did not quite know what to say to this: so she helped herself to some tea and bread-and-butter, and then turned to the Dormouse, and repeated her question. "Why did they live at the bottom of a well?"

The Dormouse again took a minute or two to think about it, and then said, "It was a treacle-well."

"There's no such thing!" Alice was beginning very angrily, but the Hatter and the March Hare went "Sh! sh!" and the Dormouse sulkily remarked, "If you can't be civil, you'd better finish the story for yourself."

"No, please go on!" Alice said very humbly; "I won't interrupt again. I dare say there may be one."

"One, indeed!" said the Dormouse indignantly. However, he consented to go on. "And so these three little sisters - they were learning to draw, you know -"

"What did they draw?" said Alice, quite forgetting her promise.

"Treacle," said the Dormouse, without considering at all this time.

"I want a clean cup," interrupted the Hatter: "let's all move one place on."

He moved on as he spoke, and the Dormouse followed him: the March Hare moved into the Dormouse's place, and Alice rather unwillingly took the place of the March Hare. The Hatter was the only one who got any advantage from the change: and Alice was a good deal worse off than before, as the March Hare had just upset the milk-jug into his plate.

Alice did not wish to offend the Dormouse again, so she began very cautiously: "But I don't understand. Where did they draw the treacle from?"

"You can draw water out of a water-well," said the Hatter; "so I should think you could draw treacle out of a treacle-well - eh, stupid?"

"But they were in the well," Alice said to the Dormouse, not choosing to notice this last remark.

"Of course they were," said the Dormouse; "- well in."

This answer so confused poor Alice, that she let the Dormouse go on for some time without interrupting it.

"They were learning to draw," the Dormouse went on, yawning and rubbing its eyes, for it was getting very sleepy; "and they drew all manner of things - everything that begins with an M -"

"Why with an M?" said Alice.

"Why not?" said the March Hare.

Alice was silent.

The Dormouse had closed its eyes by this time, and was going off into a doze; but, on being pinched by the Hatter, it woke up again with a little shriek, and went on: "- that begins with an M, such as mouse-traps, and the moon, and memory, and muchness - you know you say things are "much of a muchness"- did you ever see such a thing as a drawing of a muchness?"

"Really, now you ask me," said Alice, very much confused, "I don't think -"

"Then you shouldn't talk," said the Hatter.

This piece of rudeness was more than Alice could bear: she got up in great disgust, and walked off; the Dormouse fell asleep instantly, and neither of the others took the least notice of her going, though she looked back once or twice, half hoping that they would call after her: the last time she saw them, they were trying to put the Dormouse into the teapot.

"At any rate I'll never go there again!" said Alice as she picked her way through the wood. "It's the stupidest tea-party I ever was at in all my life!"

Just as she said this, she noticed that one of the trees had a door leading right into it. "That's very curious!" she thought. "But everything's curious today. I think I may as well go in at once." And in she went.

Once more she found herself in the long hall, and close to the little glass table. "Now, I'll manage better this time," she said to herself, and began by taking the little golden key, and unlocking the door that led into the garden. Then she went to work nibbling at the mushroom (she had kept a piece of it in her pocket) till she was about a foot high: then she walked down the little passage: and then - she found herself at last in the beautiful garden, among the bright flower-beds and the cool fountains.*

"The mad cow's gone and done it," she screeched as I rushed on into the room.

Klaxon, klaxon, klaxon, klaxon, klaxon, klaxon, klaxon.

I stood on a screw that was lying on the floor; it embedded itself in my heel.

"Jesus, fucking, Christ Almighty." I hopped up and down on one leg.

"What ..? When ..? Who?" I screamed, as I twirled on the spot like a Whirling Dervish, then spun across the floor to a chair. Thud.

"What's going on?" I asked, as I pulled the thing from my foot.

"That bitch Thatcher," spat Joyce. "That's the Poll Tax in place … And as usual we're the clowns … She's finally imposed the Poll Tax, and we're the fucking clowns … We always knew it was her intention to introduce it in Scotland first … Jesus, fucking, Christ Almighty … We're the fucking clowns … She might as well have given us all a running-wheel and been done with it, or a run-about ball. Because that's all we are to that lot down south; fucking guinea pigs."

> *Scots, wha hae wi' Wallace bled,*
> *Scots, wham Bruce has aften led;*
> *Welcome to your gory bed,*
> *Or to victory!*

"Cunt! That's what she is Ellis. A fucking cunt. And today of all days."

I could hear the distain in her voice, and as she continued to spout her vitriol, spit was flying from her mouth.

"The hatred I have for that woman is incalculable," she said. "I'm only sorry the IRA didn't finish what they started and saved us all a lot of trouble. Hanging's much to good for that bitch, I hope she burns in hell."

Shoo! I hadn't seen her like this before. This was a first for me.

I'd heard her rant about Thatcher and the Tories, but this was new. This had come from the bowels of the earth, straight up through her feet.

"Cunt.

Cunt, cunt, cunt, cunt, cunt, cunt, cunt."

I could feel an eruption about to explode. I had to get her away.

First, take her down to India, and get her to take a seat. I fancied a spot of shikantaza may do the trick. She'd been sitting for almost a year now, on and off, and studying zen texts from the cabinet. So, if anything was likely to alter the mood she was in, I considered it likely to be that. Get her down and sit her on the zafu while I worked out what to do.

Come up with a plan to bring her back down and get her on an even keel.

Got it.

I loaded the panniers then strapped them on the back of the bike along with the tent and sleeping bags. I then raided the cellar for canned goods and noodles. Lifted the binoculars from the table at the door, placed them in the sidecar, returned to the cottage, switched off the tele then dressed.

By the time Joyce returned from sitting shikantaza, I could see she was a whole lot calmer than she had been, and I was sure I could detect a smile on her countenance. Which all in all was a good thing. A calmer mood for the day ahead and hopefully into the night. Her mind away from the Ugly Woman and on to things more wholesome.

I was standing by the door in my leathers and boots when she looked me straight in the eye.

"Gate gate paragate parasamgate bodhi svaha.

Where are we going?" she asked, then grinned.

"Come on," I said. "Let's go.

Grab your jacket and put on shoes. Your chariot awaits at the door."

By two o'clock we were travelling south-west on a course for the Galloway Forest Park, where a night under the stars would hopefully, as I'd intimated earlier, remove Mrs. Thatcher from her consciousness once and for all. As focused on the Pleiades or some such, she'd be more inclined to concentrate on that rather than the news of the day, which in retrospect would be of no significance in comparison when looked at in perspective.

We prepared the ground then put up the tent. This was going to be good.

"The sky will be clear tonight," I said. "According to the weather forecast. According to that it's to be clear for a week, so we should be able to see the stars, and it is feasible we might catch a glimpse of a satellite."

And the stars we saw in great profusion, clear across the sky.

"There," she said, "to the left a bit. Below Orion."

I didn't have a clue as to what I was looking for, then once I got my bearings, in that great expanse of dome, my eye was pressed firmly to the scope. Joyce, director of communications, relaying directions to my ear. "There."

A meteor suddenly traversed our field of vision then disappeared into the night.

"Wow."

Another then another then another then another then another then another then another.

We watched in awe for a good ten minutes then Joyce turned to face me.

"Interplanetary junk," she said. "That's all it really is."

Next morning being Sunday as it was, we made up our mind, or rather Joyce did, that as we were in the vicinity we should call on The Fish People. Friends she'd made in her days campaigning for the CND and who now, through luck and a whole load of jiggery-pokery, were living in Badnoch, having managed to purchase a small, one bedroom cottage as soon as it came to the market.

Like I said, it was Sunday, so turning up early was out of the question, as according to Joyce they always attended church in the morning, service eleven-thirty.

In the meantime, we'd head for Wigtown where we'd scour the second-hand book shops for anything I could find by Shelley or Coleridge, and whatever was available on haiku for Joyce: A type of Japanese short form poetry that works on a syllable count, if I recall correctly. She'd explained it to me on numerous occasions in the past. That's as much as I knew; It was all to do with syllable count. Five, seven, five.

We made breakfast, broke camp, packed the bike then left.

Twenty minutes later we were parked on the Vennel, walking toward South Main.

The Portable Coleridge was soon in my grasp, a sturdy, solid, weighty volume, published in the USA.

The haiku proved more elusive, and in the end, we abandoned the idea. Basho a bit too far for a bookshop Sunday in Wigtown, where the word of the Lord assured it only ever the nonreligious owner to be open on such a day. The bells that called to morning service ignored over cups of tea.

One was tracing Arabic as we walked in through his door.

"Basho? Don't think I've heard of him. Try Connolley's up the road."

We turned then slowly retraced our steps, rolling a cig as we went.

"Why do you call them The Fish People, Joyce?" I knew though I couldn't ...

"It's like this," she said. "When we first met - at a CND rally - they were covered in stickers and badges of The Jesus Fish symbol, either stitched to their belongings or stuck all over their car. I was intrigued and gave them the moniker, The Fish People, and that was that, it stuck. And I've known them as that ever since. Their real names - the ones given by their father who I believe was and elder in the Church of Scotland - are Miriam and Eunice Webster. Neither of them are married and having broached the subject with them from time to time, to no avail, I have no intention of doing so again. They're quite happy to be living together, Getting on with their lives."

We arrived at their door at a quarter to two. Joyce chapped the fish door knocker.

Miriam:

"Eunice, it's Joyce. She's here with Jeffery ... I think it's him."

Never having met either sister in the flesh I quite understood her doubt.

Eunice came rushing from the kitchen through the hall and brought up short at the door.

"Oh, my word, I don't believe it ... This is a sight for sore eyes."

The sisters gathered Joyce in their arms and carried her into the house. An arm each, under her knees, and Joyce's arms at their shoulders. All three of them singing the Internationale, myself bringing up the rear. They dropped her in an easy chair with a view out over the river.

"Oh my god," said Miriam to Eunice. "Can you believe this?"

"I don't believe my eyes," said Miriam. "It must be true.

We were only speaking of you a month ago, reminiscing on times past. Marches and times at camp."

"Those were the days," said Eunice in reply. "The three of us all together."

They rambled on for five, then Joyce did the introductions.

"Eunice, Miriam, this is Jeffery. Jeffery, Eunice and Miriam."

Miriam said she'd only ever heard good things about me, and likewise Eunice.

"Every time we speak on the phone," said Miriam, "Joyce always mentions you, and tells us what's going on. It's always good to hear how the two of you are doing and be kept in the picture. Pleased to meet you at last," she said, then reached out and shook my hand. Eunice did likewise, and said it was an honour, kissed me on the side of the cheek.

"Afternoon tea all round?" she asked. "Miriam's been busy baking."

A better welcome was never surpassed. And before we knew it, we were furnished, with what I can only describe as the best afternoon tea; a three tier stand and all.

Cucumber sandwiches, butter and salt. Honey roast ham with mustard. All with crust removed to perfection, small triangles and rounds. Then came the scones with clotted cream and jam, followed by Battenberg cake. Half a dozen macarons, Victoria sponge, tasty shortbread cookies.

Then after we had eaten, I retired to the couch and lifted an Etch A Sketch. The girls chatted on where they sat at the table until it was time to leave. I drew a picture of a man in a boat whilst the girls reminisced the past.

Before sunset we climbed aboard then started our journey home.

Work in the morning was a damper and it played on our minds. And try as we might to keep it from the fore it danced like a demon in the night.

Mondays always haunted Sundays. That's the way it was.

10

"And it all happened, just like dear old Tommy Cooper used to say: 'Just like that.'"

Back in the real world things had taken a downturn, and it was time to discuss the Poll Tax at length, then come to a decision as to what course of action to take under the prevailing circumstances, either for or against. Against. Make a stand and bring the thing to a dead-stop, buffering end.

It didn't play out like that, and in the end we were led up the garden path by people like Tommy Sheridan.

Headstrong and reckless we were, you had to stand and be counted. Show your hand and be damned as it were. See it out to the bitter end with an act of civil disobedience. Can't pay. Won't pay. Didn't pay.

There were consequences to be had.

It was all very well marching and holding hands as we walked along in unison till the end came and you were on your own. Wondering when you'd eat your next meal. Starving, starving, starving. Electricity and gas cut off at source for failure to pay. Wages arrested on a monthly basis for standing your ground.

~~Failure to pay.~~
~~Failure to pay.~~

~~Failure to pay.~~
Okay asshole we'll arrest your wages, see what you think about that.

And they did. Once a month. And we were the lucky ones. We had enough to fall back on when the initial euphoria dissipated and scattered to the four winds, and we realised we were on our own and nobody had our back.

~~Failure to pay.~~
~~Failure to pay.~~
~~Failure to pay.~~

Cut off their gas, cut off their electric. Poindings and warrants for arrest.

~~Failure to pay.~~
~~Failure to pay.~~
~~Failure to pay.~~

Ten pound for the tv set, five for the big fridge-freezer. Couch and bed a round six quid. Two for the kiddie's toys.

~~Failure to pay.~~
~~Failure to pay.~~
~~Failure to pay.~~

And as things stood, and we got deeper and deeper immersed in the mire, I was glad of Joyce's prepping cellar and the sustenance held therein. For as soon as the Sheriff had taken our wages there was little for anything else. We cooked by camp stove and read by candlelight, marched on a protest when we could.

~~Failure to pay.~~
~~Failure to pay.~~
~~Failure to pay.~~

Five year later and the struggle continued, a reminder of our failure to pay.

11

It looked as if we weren't getting out the bit, our only saving grace the lack of a mortgage. All praise be to gran. For if it hadn't been for her generosity and leaving Joyce the house when she died, god knows where we'd have ended up, and it doesn't bear thinking about. The unpleasantries eviction would have involved, had it come to that, which I've no doubt, looking back on the situation now it would have, killer at minimum. For us it was only gas and electric they cut, and we managed to live with that. Paying them back was a long slow process and they wanted their pound of flesh.

Five year later we were still in the grip of crippling fiscal penury, and in the interim had been led to war in Iraq by John Major after Thatcher oversaw the build-up of troops in Saudi Arabia before being forced to resign her position as Prime Minister after she returned from an EU summit meeting in Brussels.

Any hope her successor would distance himself from the war mongering of George H W Bush was seen to be pie in the sky, when on the 17th of January 1991 they initiated Desert Storm.

The organ grinder had called the tune and we danced atop the piano.

"Fucking American bastards," said Joyce, "They only have to say jump. The puppet master pulls the strings, and we jerk along like fools.

When will the madness end, Ellis? When will it come to an end?"

In the school of political projectors, I was but ill entertained; the professors appearing, in my judgment, wholly out of their senses, which is a scene that never fails to make me melancholy. These unhappy people were proposing schemes for persuading monarchs to choose favourites upon the score of their wisdom, capacity, and virtue; of teaching ministers to consult the public good; of rewarding merit, great abilities, eminent services; of instructing princes to know their true interest, by placing it on the same foundation with that of their people; of choosing for employments persons qualified to exercise them, with many other wild, impossible chimeras, that never entered before into the heart of man to conceive; and confirmed in me the old observation, "that there is nothing so extravagant and irrational, which some philosophers have not maintained for truth."

But, however, I shall so far do justice to this part of the Academy, as to acknowledge that all of them were not so visionary. There was a most ingenious doctor, who seemed to be perfectly versed in the whole nature and system of government. This illustrious person had very usefully employed his studies, in finding out effectual remedies for all diseases and corruptions to which the several kinds of public administration are subject, by the vices or infirmities of those who govern, as well as by the licentiousness of those who are to obey. For instance: whereas all writers and reasoners have agreed, that there is a strict universal resemblance between the natural and the political body; can there be any thing more evident, than that the health of both must be preserved, and the diseases cured, by the same prescriptions? It is allowed, that senates and great councils are often troubled with redundant, ebullient, and other peccant humours; with many diseases of the head, and more of the heart; with strong convulsions, with grievous contractions of the nerves and sinews in both hands, but especially the right; with spleen, flatus, vertigos, and deliriums; with scrofulous tumours, full of fetid purulent matter; with sour frothy ructations: with canine appetites, and crudeness of digestion, besides many others, needless to mention. This doctor therefore proposed, "that upon the meeting of the senate, certain physicians should attend it the three first days of their sitting, and at the close of each day's debate feel the pulses of every senator; after which, having maturely considered and consulted upon the nature of the several maladies, and the methods of cure, they should on the fourth day return to the senate house, attended by their apothecaries stored with proper medicines; and before the members sat, administer to each of them lenitives, aperitives, abstersives, corrosives, restringents, palliatives, laxatives, cephalalgics, icterics, apophlegmatics, acoustics, as their several cases required; and, according as *these medicines should operate, repeat, alter, or omit them, at the next meeting."**

I couldn't answer her question. I found it confusing, and my brain hurt.

"What if there is no end? You know, when we die and things don't get any better, and it's one continuous round of misery. Life death life death life death life. For all we know that could be the case. The occasional five minutes of pleasure here and there then mostly misery. Up until now that's the case. We're riding on a high now and then, only to be brought back down with a bang, for reasons without our control. Taxes, price hikes and a severe lack of finances. And those, finances, are always at the back of people's mind. They can't get on, and it's through no fault of their own. Then opposition parties have a cheek to blah their shite and tell us we'd be better off if they were in power to get our vote. Then once in … It's a blame culture, politics, Joyce. I don't know why we bother."

"I understand your concern," she said. "I don't see it in such black and white terms as yourself. You have to vote, that's the bottom line. I know we don't always get what we like, but if you don't use your vote then you don't have a say. You're not participating. You have to exercise your right or you're not in it. Moaning about whoever the hell's in power when you don't like their policies and the way they're running the country, and you haven't bothered your arse to vote yourself doesn't exactly cut it. You don't have a say. That's the bottom line. You're either in or out. Sitting on the fence is not an option if you want to play your part. Vote and then you can criticize, Ellis. Then you'll be playing your part."

She was right of course, and I understood that. I also understood her desire to protest at the drop of a hat when a cause she felt strongly about presented itself and she'd take to the road, armed with appropriate banner. She'd been arrested twice in the past for her involvement in street demonstrations, and the way things stood with the political situation I envisioned it wouldn't end there.

And I was right.

By the end of November 1990, Thatcher had been ousted and the country was now being run by the unelected John Major, who by mid January had taken us to war with Iraq: Operation Desert Storm, at the prompting of his new friend Bush.

Joyce was on the march once again. I stayed home having considered, then taken on board, all she'd said concerning my refusal to vote in past elections and therefore not having a voice. I'd never seriously looked at things in the world of politics before. It was all surface moaning, and in all reality guff. I was complaining for the sake of complaining and nothing more than that.

Moan, moan, moan, moan, moan, moan, moan.

That was the depth of my political consciousness. Moan, moan, moan.

I'd need to understand things before I opened my mouth. Get my vote in the ballot box before my opinion was voiced.

Joyce left with Eunice and Miriam in their car, bound for a demo in the City. A banner in their rear-view window declaring the sentiments held by all three. STOP THE BOMBING OF IRAQ.

I took the time they were gone to finish the Coleridge book I had bought.

12

Over the years nothing changed as the rich got richer and the poor struggled along.

It was always on the cards, or they'd like you to believe it was, that things will get better, and the less well offs situation will improve, and we'd all be living in utopia.

We'd heard it before - especially when an election was imminent - the need to believe things would change in the mind of the idealist, and were worth holding on to, albeit an illusion. Nothing more than a pipe dream.

As soon as the next round of votes came up, I was putting my **X** on the page. I had taken what Joyce had said on board and determined that if I was going to shout about those in the seat of government, passing laws that affected all aspects of our lives, then I should put pen to paper to have my say. Say what I liked without the rebuttal, 'You don't vote.'

I'd start with the local elections at first then move myself up from their.

I didn't expect to wait another seven years for the Tories to finally collapse.
X.

"Beautiful Soup, so rich and green,
Waiting in a hot tureen!

Who for such dainties would not stoop?
Soup of the evening, beautiful Soup!
Soup of the evening, beautiful Soup!
  Beau--ootiful Soo--oop!
  Beau--ootiful Soo--oop!
Soo--oop of the e--e--evening,
  Beautiful, beautiful Soup!

"Beautiful Soup! Who cares for fish,
Game, or any other dish?
Who would not give all else for two
pennyworth only of beautiful Soup?
Pennyworth only of beautiful Soup?
  Beau--ootiful Soo--oop!
  Beau--ootiful Soo--oop!
Soo--oop of the e--e--evening,
  Beautiful, beauti--FUL SOUP!"

("Soo—oop of the e—e—evening,
  Beautiful, beautiful Soup!")*

*

BOOK THREE

*

And we knew he was the Deil by his glaring red eyes.

1

We started to see a lot more of Eunice and Miriam during the 90s, either through our visits to Badnoch, which I came to love, as it let me exercise my passion for second-hand book buying by taking trips to Wigtown on the bike whenever we were there, and spend an hour rummaging in the hope I'd find what I was looking for. Or the times they'd visit up here.

And when we did catch up with each other politics was always to the fore.

"We can say one thing in Major's favour," said Eunice, as we sat at the table drinking wine. "He got rid of the Poll Tax. I can't say this new-fangled Council Tax is going to fare any better. The jury's still out on that one as far as it goes. We'll have to wait and see."

Miriam played QANAT as an opening word on the Scrabble board for twenty-eight.

"And don't forget The Citizen's Charter," said Joyce, then turned up her eyes.

"Miriam said she couldn't believe it. "Where's the money coming from? It's all very well implementing the thing, but when they then reduce the money, they said was going to be available, what's the point?

Typical Tory ploy."

Joyce played an I to the Q for eleven then drew a tile from the bag.

"It makes you laugh," she said, as she placed the tile on her rack.

"And what's all this nonsense about back to basics and traditional family shit? There's only one place that lot would like to send us and that's back to Victorian times and values. Send your children up a chimney and doff your cap when they pass. It's all lip service, and as soon as we get to grips with that the better."

Eunice played out from the right of the N for a triple letter on an I. NAIL.

"I don't know when it'll end," said Joyce. "They've been in power forever. You'd think the country would be thoroughly disgusted by the way they're running things and the state the place is in. There's an air of acceptance about it. It's as if people have become apathetic with the entire system and the way things are run. Sure, there are the likes of us who take to the streets and make our feelings known, but the vast majority of people are sitting at home glued to their tv set filling their heads with drivel such as soap operas and Question Time. Have you ever watched that? Same drivel week in, week out, and no one answers a question. It should be called avoidance time the way they skirt about issues. Either that or they blame it on the opposition. Same crap each week."

LOVE.

I could only vision Major swinging about on a trapeze in a leopard-print jacket and white glove on Spitting Image, and I couldn't get it out of my head.

"My father was in the circus, you know."

The girls replied, "We know."

They got my sense of humour, and I wasn't speaking to myself.

Joyce got to her feet then walked to a unit, removed a menu from its drawer.

"Chinkie?" she said, as she opened it. "How about the set meal for four? I feel quite hungry. Anyone else? Ellis will go on the bike."

The girls both drew her a look of distain before they said to her in unison, *"Joyce."*

"Sorry for that," she said in return. "He keeps telling me the same."

Forty minutes later I was standing in Lim's, placing my order with May, where a short conversation concerning her family back in the Philippines and how she was doing herself took place, in the way of passing time.

She told me her sister and mother were still awaiting visas that would permit them to travel and grant them residency. All being well, she said, she hoped they'd be here by the end of the year, and they could live as a family again. She hadn't seen either of them in over four year and it would be nice to be reunited. She was hopeful, she said, that once they were here the government would allow them to stay. All going well, and their visas issued, she couldn't see why not.

I thanked her for my order then left. Twenty minutes later I was back in the house clearing a space on the table.

"Right," I said. "I'll lay it out on the table here. Help yourselves."

I untied the bag then removed the trays, their content written on the lids:

Large barbecue spare ribs. Sweet and sour chicken. Duck with pineapple. King prawn with mushroom. Beef chop suey. Special foo young. Special fried rice. Chinese roast pork on beansprouts with barbecue sauce.

Joyce brought in knives and forks, spoons and kitchen roll. Beer, plates, a bottle of water. A carton of apple juice.

"Did we not get any free prawn crackers? We usually do."

I looked for them, then it suddenly dawned I'd left them lying in the sidecar.

"Back in a tick," I said, as I turned, then left to go retrieve.

I also brought in four new menus I'd lifted from the side of the till.

"Here."

Everyone spooned food onto their plate, stretching to reach a dish.

"Here," said Eunice, "this sounds good. We could order this next time.

Black pepper beef ... Tender pieces of beef fried with black pepper, onions and mixed bell peppers. Soy sauce and cooking wine ... I'd like that."

"Sounds good to me," said Miriam.

"How about the Kung pao chicken?" said Joyce. "Famous Sichuan-style ... Diced chicken, dried chili, cucumber, fried cashews ... Mmm."

I said I'd go for the sweet and sour pork, if ordering for myself.

Miriam said it was hot pot for her, especially if eating in-house.

"The Lepak Santai Steamboat and Grill in Ipoh?" she said to Eunice … "Best Tom Yam I've tasted. If you're ever in Malaysia, you should give it a go. Ipoh itself is a lovely place. One of the best destinations we've been on our travels. I'd like to go back."

Eunice concurred with her sister's observation and said she'd return herself.

"Beautiful place altogether," she said. "And one I'd return to tomorrow. The Ipoh white coffee is to die for. They roast the beans with palm oil and serve it with condensed milk. That, and the ice balls served in the old town covered in flavoured syrup."

"And the temples," said Miriam. "Buddhist. A lot of them are in caves. You should go. A truly beautiful place."

VEX

XI

LATE

"I'd like to go, and I think Joyce would be up for it. I doubt it will happen, all the same. I was informed yesterday there's talk about closing the warehouse. From what I've heard they're considering relocating to Liverpool. Nothing conclusive. Only rumour. I wouldn't like to hold my breath all the same."

Joyce looked shocked, as this was the first she'd heard about it.

"You forgot to mention it to me," she said. "Why didn't you tell me?"

GIRL

JAR
HANG
TITHE

FAT
DOTE
FUNNY

"I didn't tell you," I said, "because I haven't heard anything concrete. As far as it goes it's only rumour, and up until I hear anything to the contrary that's all it will be. Up until the management put out a statement either denying or verifying they're relocating south then nothing's set in stone. It didn't make any sense to cause you worry if, indeed, it is only rumour. What would have been the sense in that? So up until I heard one way or another, I was keeping my mouth shut. It sort of slipped out there, that's all. It must have been on my mind."

She looked at me a second or two, and then she said, "I get it. I get exactly what you mean, because now it's on my mind too. It'll now be there until we discover if they're actually moving or not. Shit."

Miriam said it was a prime example of the English looking after themselves. "They're probably only here," she said, "due to government grants - pushed as an incentive - that lasts five year, and now it's run its course. Time to move back home. Bye-bye. Take their money and run. Happens all the time. They dangle the carrot to get companies to relocate north of the boarder, then once they do their allocated time and the money's in the bank they pack up and leave. Move their entire show back south, lock, stock and barrel. It's a bind, and one I don't see we can do anything about except for breaking away. And there in lies our quandary.

Over the past six month we've been toying with the idea of changing our vote from Labour to SNP. Sounds an easy thing to do, rationally speaking. Not that easy for us."

BANKED

"No." said Eunice, "it's not. We were raised under the Labour banner by our parents and grandparents, so to change allegiance now - right when it looks like the Tories are about to be ousted - would be like a stab in the back to them. We've discussed it at length and come to the conclusion SNP's the way to go. If not independence right away, then a devolved parliament to get us there in the end. We're definitely advocating a switch. We see it as the only way.

It's worth thinking about," she said. "when they're closing our industries."

I reached for more of the king prawn mushroom, pork with barbecue sauce.

"I haven't looked at it like that before," said Joyce, "and like yourselves, SNP is not a party I considered. They're not on my radar. They're maybe worth thinking about all the same. It might be time we took matters into our own hands and plumped for independence. It couldn't be any worse than things are under the Tories. I still think I'd vote Labour to see what they do for us, then take it from there. You just don't know, they might be the jab in the arm the country needs. Only time will tell."

Eunice helped herself to special foo young, beansprouts, and special fried rice.

YES/IS

Joyce made coffee then the girls gave a hand to remove the empty dishes from the room. They put the containers in the kitchen bin, knives and forks in the sink.

"Oh, I like those," said Eunice, when she saw the paintings by Jules on the wall. "Unusual."

Miriam looked and was likewise smitten. "Where did you get those?" she asked.

"A friend of ours painted them," said Joyce. "We first met them at Lannion … David and Rosa from our days campaigning at Faslane? Their place down in Britanny."

"Ah, David and Rosa," said the girls in unison, looking one another in the eye. "Those were happy days."

"I miss them," said Miriam. "How are they anyway?"

"Fine," answered Joyce. "They're doing pretty well, running a lovely set-up down there. A sort of B and B type place catering mostly to naturists. Anyway, that's where we met Jules and Lena, and it was Jules that painted the pictures. Well, De Führer. He painted that when we were there and had got to know them, and as soon as we saw it we made an offer. We were attracted to it, and the method he used to apply the paint caught us as rather unusual. He painted it using his cock and balls rather than using brushes."

Eunice moved in for a closer look, followed by her sister at her back.

"He did a fantastic job. I love the shape of his nose."

Miriam turned to look at Maggie. "He's definitely done a job here. Her head reminds me of a great big arse, and her hair's like candy floss."

Joyce laughed at that, then told her she'd specifically asked she look like that, and he was happy to oblige.

"Done a fantastic job, and Lena wrote the poem."

She pointed to the verse, inside the frame, which sat between the paintings.

"Maggie and the poem were both done here when the came to visit."

Eunice read the poem to herself, out loud, ruminated then said, "Interesting."

Back at the table we continued the game we'd left to tidy up.

YORE

"You see, that's the trouble with eating Chinese food ... half an hour later you're hungry again."

Miriam and Eunice concurred.

"We thought it us," said Eunice, in reply. "We always find it the same. Half an hour after you gobble it up your belly's rumbling for more."

"Feed me, feed me, feed me," said Miriam.

Laughter filled the room.

VERSE

"I don't know what it is, but if we have pizza or Indian we're always full for ages.

ARC/AS - blank an A.

"Could be the MSG."

"Possibly," said Joyce, "I haven't considered it before: post-Chinese food hunger and how it materializes."

I watched as the cogs went off in her head and knew she was thinking hard.

"I'm not so sure sodium would necessarily have that effect," she said. "I'd be more inclined to say it's linked to a lack of potatoes - which have a high satiety value - in their meals."

VOG

"And rice raises your blood sugar level quite rapidly which, in itself, can lead to a crash, leaving you feeling hungry again. So, I don't know, take your pick. Entirely up to yourselves."

I didn't have a clue as to what they were talking about so kept my mouth shut, it didn't affect me like that. I was stuffed once I'd ate my fill, and it usually lasted all night. Chinese, Indian, it made no difference; pizza or Turkish kebab. Once I'd shovelled it in it normally stayed for the night. Only ever moving after coffee in the morning initiated toilet call.

JET

"Are you still in contact with Rene?" enquired Eunice. "We tried to get in touch with her a while back to no avail. Do you know if she's still alive?"

BORN

Joyce poured another round of drinks, then said she'd heard she'd died.

"As far as I'm led to believe she died about a year and a half ago. I was speaking with Orla Hennessey - remember her? - and when I brought her name up, she informed me she was dead. Breast cancer.

According to Orla they caught it too late, and they couldn't save her. She was only forty-two. A husband and four kids she left behind. She was such a nice person too."

"Yes, she was," said Miriam. "If you required help, she was always there. First to lend a hand."

"She came out and picked me up when the car broke down one night," said Miriam. "Eleven o'clock in the pouring rain, Orla was there for me."

"She was like that," said Joyce. "Nothing was too much trouble. You could always count on Orla."

LOVE
TIED
RUDE

PEG
AW/AWE

"We got to know her through our involvement with the CND," said Miriam, "and liked her straight away. She had that type of personality you warmed to immediately, and we never heard anyone say a bad word against her all the time we knew her. That's how it goes, it's always the good go young. Gees, four kids, it doesn't bear thinking about; Mike's got a job on his hands."

WE

She then relayed information of a planned trip they were making to Iona in the Inner Hebrides in a week's time to visit the abbey - the home of Gaelic monasticism for over three hundred years - and spend a bit of time on the island: A Friday to Monday sort of thing. They'd already made a reservation at one of the family run bed and breakfast establishments, and all going according to plan would take their time and study the abbeys fine architecture in detail, then time permitting, visit the ruins of the Augustinian nunnery which was dissolved shortly after the Reformation and fell to ruin.

They'd cross by ferry from Oban to Craignure, then once on Mull another ferry from Fionnphort to Iona.

The two full days they'd spend on the island more than ample.

WE
GROUT
WAIT
EM/MO
BUS - blank a U

RUE
TI
CHIS/IS
Final play, FIT

They left on Sunday at ten o'clock, after bacon and eggs.

2

It was a first, and something I didn't envision likely to happen under the Tories. I was redundant.

The word itself was repugnant with all it's connotations of expiry date. And cognizant it was the job - or one's role within the company itself - that was redundant, rather than the person employed to conduct the task no longer required, didn't soften the blow. I was redundant and that was that. Fucking, shitting, redundant.

Redundant
Redundant
Redundant
Redundant
Fucking, shitting, redundant.

And I couldn't fathom what was next on the cards. For now, I was fucking redundant.

"You know, Joyce," I said, as we packed the bike for a trip to the coast. "We're only a commodity, and that's all we'll ever be. Once we've served our purpose that's that. Once they're done with us, they throw us on the heap and leave us to breakdown like compost, then once we're mulch that's it.

Think about it Joyce, redundant. It's an obnoxious word in itself.

And as for the struggles it brings, as far as the government's concerned, they're non-existent. All they're doing is setting us against each other and making a damn good job of it into the bargain. We're invisible to them Joyce. Invisible."

I threw the panniers on the back of the bike then we headed off north for Fife.

Back home I began applying for as many jobs as I could and all without success. Ninety-nine per cent of those I did apply for, the company advertising the position didn't have the decency or curtesy to reply, either to say they had taken receipt of the application and that, unfortunately, I was unsuccessful, or to say they had received it.

Then Joyce was made redundant when they closed the business and blamed it on the out-of-town shopping park, stating that since that opened, staying abreast of the large multi national's prices was proving an impossible task. And in the end, they beat them down to where they could no longer compete.

As from Monday the business was closed. Another eleven on the dole.

"Well, that's the end of the good old days when you could walk out of one job and straight into another without any problem," I said to Joyce, as I opened the paper at the situations vacant then spread it out on the table.

She came in from the living room and filled the kettle, turned the grill to HIGH.

"Looks like it," she said. "The only saving grace is we've still got money in the bank from what was left us by gran - although that did take a bit of a beating during the Poll Tax debacle when they arrested our wages and forced us to delve into it to pay for gas and electricity - and your redundancy money; Though that was a pittance. And the storeroom is still well stocked. Things will be fine.

Toast?"

She laid four slice of bread on the griddle then slid it into the grill.

"All you can do is keep applying. You'll get there in the end. I'll get a position in Morrison's or Asda, they're always looking for staff."

She laid out butter, a pot of jam, a tub of Gentleman's Relish.

I heard the rattle of the letter box so got up to collect the mail:

A painting of Hitler's Goldenes Parteiabzeichen (number 7) rendered in coloured inks as a yoyo with string, on a plain white A6 postcard.

On the back left side a poem by Lena, opposite the address of our cottage.

It sold for
40,000 Deutsche Mark,
the purchaser
walking the dog.
  Hier Blondi,
Gassi.
      Lena

I showed it to Joyce who studied it a while then propped it against the jam jar.

"You've got to love them," she said, as she spread relish on buttered toast. "Bangers; Life wouldn't be the same if we were all alike, now would it?"

"We should take a trip over on the bike. They'd like to see us."

Six month later I was working at SKY Television, employed through an external agency company who skimmed what they could from the top of my wage for the pleasure of finding me work. It was all I could get, and all going well I was assured that after six month - and with a clean nose - employment with SKY proper was a distinct possibility. And if you believed that you'd believe whatever they told you. I went along with it. There was a need for money. And who knew, at the end of the six month, like they said, permanent employment would be assured and all our troubles behind us. I dipped in a toe then jumped; working away in an office.

Shit; that was a first. And not a first I anticipated. I never expected to see myself working in an office environment, as I didn't consider myself office material. If anyone told me, a year or two prior, I'd be donning a suit and tie to go to work I might have laughed. There you have it.

Six month later I was full-time, and Joyce was on the tills in Asda.

Benefits and holidays were now in hand along with SKY TV.

3

Now was the time to act ... Utilize my vote.

Major called a general election on 17 March 1997, ensuring a long formal campaign as the election wasn't scheduled until 1 May to coincide with the local elections that were taking place on the same day. And as the populace, on a whole, were pretty much done with the Conservatives, it was more or less expected that Labour would win with a landslide majority, which they duly did. And after eighteen year of Tory rule the country decided to party.

I wasn't so sure.

Joyce switched allegiance to SNP as she said she might; and I, for the first time, utilized my **X** by placing it in the box next to Labour, thinking it'd make a difference and we'd all be living off champagne and caviar the minute they took over. How stupid was I? Expecting roses and chocolate box scenes, the land exuding perfume. Mug. And I mean that most sincerely here. What a fucking stupid mug.

 How naïve must I have been to think that replacing one set of assholes with another was going to make a difference, when they're all tarred with the same brush and only in it for themselves. I'd already told Joyce we were a commodity to them and here I was putting pen to paper in the hope that things would change.

Eighteen year of Conservative rule had come to an end, and here we were sitting on the cusp of a new millennium where anything was possible, and the future looked bright. Labour, for all their unknowns, were punting themselves to us as a universal placebo, and I for one was taken in.

I wanted better than was gone, and ended up with Blair, who took us into a war in Afghanistan that dragged on forever.

What a fucking ass wipe he was; after his ass was licked:

"Form an orderly queue there please. Tickets dispatched at the bar."

Eddie Izzard, Lenny Henry, Helen Mirren, and Noel.

That was the point I thought to myself, What the hell have I done?

That was the point I knew that their propaganda machine had begun.

"Hardly in power," I said to Joyce, "and that's them already at it."

She laughed.

"What did you expect?" she said, as she turned the tv to channel four. "Flowers and rainbows? They're all as bad as one another. They're only in it for what they can get. Take, take, take."

"I understand that," I said. "I expected it to be different this time. That was one of the reasons I was all for using my vote rather than let it go to waste. That and like you said, you don't have a say in things unless you vote; At this moment I'm not so confident in that assessment. It's a crock, Joyce. Wait and see."

"You should have voted SNP then. The girls were right. If we don't give it a go, we'll always be stuck in the same old rut. Labour, Tory, Labour … Vote SNP and pray for independence. It's our only hope. Then if we are lucky enough to achieve our goal, we won't get steamrollered again. And if we do, it'll be by our own kind and not some clown in Westminster. You know what I think of that lot, Ellis; Dribblers of lies."

I knew it. I knew she was right. As soon as I saw that 'Cool Brittania' shite going down in Downing Street, I knew she was right. I knew they had us exactly where they wanted us, and were laughing up their sleeve the entire time, at how easy it is to deceive us. Tell the diddies what they want to hear, and they'll vote for us.

"I'm not saying we'd be better off if we did gain independence, but if we don't give it a go we won't know, one way or the other."

Too late now, I was stuck with my choice and knew I had wasted my vote.

Still, I had my say, and that was the one thing I could say I'd gained from placing my **X** in that box.

4

Back in full-time employment we were able to start building the bank balance again. And what with getting free tv as part of my contract deal with SKY Television, things were looking a whole lot brighter. We were the lucky ones. We didn't have a mortgage to worry about, due to gran's generosity in leaving her cottage to Joyce, when she died. So, all things considered, to say we were living our best life was more or less an accurate assessment, for the time being. We knew it could all crumble at any given moment, as things have a habit of doing, as soon as you start to get comfortable. Never let complacency in, it'll jump up and bite you in the ass.

You had to have eyes in the back of your head to keep up with what was going on, or before you knew it they'd be hitting you with a new tax.

Tax their fuel. Tax their booze. Tax their cigarettes.

Those are a few of their favourite things.

I recalled a saying of Joyce's: All life is suffering. Try as I may I couldn't recall exactly what it was related to; Zen I suspected. But for reasons I couldn't explain to myself I couldn't pin it down to that. I'd have to await her return from work then ask her about it then.

For now I'd make a sandwich or two, then chill on the couch for a while.

I searched the cupboards in the kitchen for five then opted for rancher's eggs, or as Joyce liked to call them when she made them, "Huevos Rancheros, they're Mexican."

In no time at all I had settled to the strains of Dylan's Desire; lifted the copy of Conrad's Victory I was almost half way through, and was lying on the couch with my eggs by my side that were taking their time to cool. Life didn't get any better than this. Then I trawled up suffering.

All life was suffering, I mused, interspersed with fleeting moments of happiness. It was suffering that was the dominant force, and there was no way round it. When you settled into a groove and it looked like happiness was here to stay … boom, you were made to suffer. It came in all sorts of guises and was failproof. You could bet your bottom dollar as soon as you settled into the old happiness routine, suffering was right at its back. Hey, you've been happy for far too long, it's time you were made to suffer. And it wasn't fussy as to how it presented itself either. Take your pick, there's a billion ways that suffering can show its face.

I lifted my bowl of eggs from the floor along with my fork and spoon. Picked up in Victory from where I'd left off as Dylan sang Black Diamond Bay.

"Joyce ... All life is suffering. Where did you get that from and what's it about? Has it to do with zen? I vaguely recall it had to do with that. Am I right?"

She removed her jacket and hung it on the peg attached to the back of the door. I followed her into the kitchen.

"Yes, it's the noble eightfold path," she said, as she went to fill the kettle. "It deals with the manner in which you do away with suffering and gain liberation from Samsara and the painful cycle of rebirth."

"Wow," I said at that point. "Exactly what's Samsara?"

"In simple terms it's the endless cycle of birth, death, and rebirth.

Anyway, to get back to what I was saying. All you have to do to escape a life of suffering is follow the noble eightfold path. That's how easy it is. When the Buddha left his palace to live the life of an ascetic and search for enlightenment, he was met on the outside by things he hadn't witnessed before as a result of his sheltered upbringing. Then, from what he witnessed there he drew the conclusion that all life is suffering, and immediately set about trying to find a means to obviate it."

She handed me a freshly poured cup of coffee then I rolled a cigarette.

"He tried self-mortification and arduous yogic practises to no avail, then after six year sat under a tree in mindful meditation until the answer came to him. Then, on his first sermon after his enlightenment, concerning the middle way, impermanence and Dependent Origination, he laid out the path to end suffering once and for all."

"And that's what they call the eightfold path?"

"The noble eightfold path:

Right view.

Right thought.

Right speech.

Right action,

Right livelihood.

Right effort.

Right mindfulness.

And right concentration."

At this point I was struggling to take it in. It felt like a full-on tsunami.

"So, if I follow the noble eightfold path that should bring an end to suffering?"

"What suffering?"

"The suffering that attaches itself to us on a daily basis. You know the sort of thing. Anxiety and depression. Worry about work. Worry about bills. The day to day struggle life brings. Drought, famine and war."

"There is no suffering."

"Then why did you say in the past that all life is suffering?"

"Because it is."

"Hell, Joyce. There's a lot of contradictions," I said.

"You're over thinking it. It's really not that difficult.

Remember The Heart Sutra?"

"Yes."

"Well, you should have stuck with it. As I told you at the time, The Heart Sutra explains everything there is to know on the subject. Give it another go. You never know. You might get the answer you're looking for. As it points out, rather clearly, in no uncertain terms, there is no suffering."

This was beginning to sound like quantum physics, and once again I was struggling to keep abreast. I wondered there were any Buddhist's at all if this was the sort of thing they had to contend with.

"There must be. It's all you see. Everywhere you look people are struggling. So, to tell me now …"

"The Heart Sutra, Ellis. The Heart Sutra. Everything you need to know is in there. It's all to do with Emptiness, and if you can get that then your on to a winner.

Therefore, Shariputra, in Emptiness there is no form, sensation, perception, volition or consciousness. No eye, no ear, no nose, no tongue, no body, no mind. No shape, no sound, no smell, no taste, no feeling, no thought. There is no realm of sight, through to no realm of cognition. There is no ignorance or ending of ignorance, through to no aging and death or ending of aging and death. There is no suffering, no cause of suffering, no ending of suffering and no path. There is no wisdom and no attainment.

It's a lack of self-existence. Or to put it another way; Dependant Origination."

I was now more confused than ever and wished I hadn't asked. I'd go back and read the sutra and try to work things out.

All was well.

In 1997 the Scottish devolution referendum was put to the electorate of the country who voted in its favour. The first meeting of our new parliament took place on 12 May 1999.

One step closer to independence. I knew where my next **X** would go.

5

The Iraq war got underway on the pretence Hussein's regime possessed weapons of mass destruction which turned out to be fabrication in the end. A whole load of fucking bullshit, from the mouth of Tony Blair who, in the long run, would be seen by all and sundry for what he was; A fucking licker of ass. Favourite flavour American Bum, in particular Dubya Bush's.

Dubya Bush's
American Bum
(Brimstone flavour)

I knew I shouldn't have voted Labour as soon as I marked my paper, and this strengthened my resolve. I should have voted to keep the Tories in power or like Joyce, opted for SNP. It was beginning to make sense what she'd been saying in advocating independence, as here we were being dragged into wars with foreign powers by a government in Westminster we had absolutely no faith or interest in against our will to appease the Americans.

I don't know if we were independent, we'd ever have got involved.

Tantamount to a war crime, they should have put Blair on trial.

Then uncle Ron died. The bearer of bad news, as always, Janine, riding up in her shiny new Jaguar with her fancy new boyfriend Steve, a ships captain, working for P&O, out of Southampton.

"Still not got that phone of yours fixed," she said, as she walked through the door. "Steve, this is Joyce … Joyce, Steve … Steve, Jeffery Ellis."

We all went through to the living room where we took a seat on the couch.

"It's about uncle Ron," she started, a gleeful smile breaking out on her face as she looked to shock with her news … We already knew. We were already one step ahead of her and knew he was dead. Mum had informed us late last night, when she'd called to speak with Joyce. The phone had been reconnected months ago and only mum had been told … "He's dead."

"We know," said Joyce. "Mum informed us last night."

"And how the hell did mum inform you, when you don't have a phone?"

"We have a phone, it's connected. Sitting out there in the hall. Plus, we've got this," she pointed toward an answer machine that was sitting on the table by the wall.

"Huh. Quite the technophile, these days, eh? Why wasn't I informed?"

"Janine, you'd be the last person on the planet I'd give my number to. Even if you were the last person on the planet apart from myself. Any notion you had of coming here and shocking me with the news of uncle Ron's death has backfired. So, if you don't mind, take your new boyfriend and go. And there's no need to inform me when the funeral will be. Mum will keep me well up to date."

She left in a rage with Steve by her side, slamming the door at her back.

The funeral took place two-and-a-half weeks after his death and the snow lay heavy on the ground. It was December, and for that time of year it was unseasonably cold and we wondered, Joyce and myself, if those who were journeying from the west would get through at all. We hoped and prayed.

The service had been set for ten o'clock and by nine forty-five the hall had already filled to capacity, the coffin resting on its catafalque, open, in front of the doleful mourners.

Then out of the blue, a mind bending Dada soirée:

A body on a gurney
waiting to be cut.
A woman plays catch
with a cat.
A child with a doll
by the side of the road.
What do you think about that?

It snowed heavily the day they buried
the Old Man.
The traffic was backed-up
for miles and distant travellers,
coming in from the west,
almost didn't arrive
on time;
though not for their lack of the try.

A minister from the Church of Crazy

officiated and as mourners poured in -
as much as to take shelter from the storm
and warm their bones, as to pay their
respects to the dead - things began
to turn strange.

Strange:

A chicken in a hat made its way to the front,
turned, then whipped-out a gun.
   "Ok shitkickers, this is how it is."
Fired three shots in the air.

Horse headed girls in silk chemises
danced in the aisles - a drunken bacchanalia -
wild and out of control.
An oompah band,
at the back of the hall,
played Tomorrow Belongs to Me,
as a television set-up high in the corner
flickered to life then rolled.

A monkey in Waffen SS black
came in and shot the chicken.
   "Swine!"

By this time the mourners were
in total shock and any chance of the
ceremony passing peacefully - as
was never to be expected
under the circumstances -
seemed to have been lost forever and a day,
in a hail of feathers and shit.

Somebody kicked the simian in the nuts
Then dragged him out to the snow.

   "That little fucker deserves to be lynched
the chicken was still in the pot."

The preacher stepped forward then
opened his book, began to read aloud:
   "To everything there is a season," he said,
   "and a time to every" ... BOOM!
A circus cannon went off with a bang,
a pensioner dropped at the rear.
A woman in sexy nurse costume
administered CPR.
   "Dead before he hit the ground," she said.
   "Let's get him out of here."

   "Open the casket and throw him in.
Today it is two for one."

A body on a gurney
waiting to be cut.
A woman plays catch
with a cat.
A child with a doll
by the side of the road.
What do you think about that?

We were stunned when we got home. We'd been stunned since proceedings went tits up and whoever had dropped dead in front of the coffin had dropped dead. Not exactly what you expect to experience when attending the funeral of a loved one, or any funeral for that. That sort of thing doesn't happen round here with three feet of snow underfoot.

"Hmm."

Tristan Tzara: Dada Manifesto 1918

There is a literature that does not reach the voracious mass. It is the work of creators, issued from a real necessity in the author, produced for himself. It expresses the knowledge of a supreme egoism, in which laws wither away. Every page must explode, either by profound heavy seriousness, the whirlwind, poetic frenzy, the new, the eternal, the crushing joke, enthusiasm for principles, or by the way in which it is printed. On the one hand a tottering world in flight, betrothed to the glockenspiel of hell, on the other hand: new men. Rough, bouncing, riding on hiccups. Behind them a crippled world and literary quacks with a mania for improvement.

I say unto you: there is no beginning and we do not tremble, we are not sentimental. We are a furious Wind, tearing the dirty linen of clouds and prayers, preparing the great spectacle of disaster, fire, decomposition. We will put an end to mourning and replace tears by sirens screeching from one continent to another. Pavilions of intense joy and widowers with the sadness of poison. Dada is the signboard of abstraction; advertising and business are also elements of poetry.

I destroy the drawers of the brain and of social organization: spread demoralization wherever I go and cast my hand from heaven to hell, my eyes from hell to heaven, restore the fecund wheel of a universal circus to objective forces and the imagination of every individual.

Philosophy is the question: from which side shall we look at life, God, the idea or other phenomena. Everything one looks at is false. I do not consider the relative result more important than the choice between cake and cherries after dinner. The system of quickly looking at the other side of a thing in order to impose your opinion indirectly is called dialectics, in other words, haggling over the spirit of fried potatoes while dancing method around it. If I cry out:

Ideal, ideal, ideal,
-Knowledge, knowledge, knowledge,
-Boomboom, boomboom, boomboom,

I have given a pretty faithful version of progress, law, morality and all other fine qualities that various highly intelligent men have discussed in so many books, only to conclude that after all everyone dances to his own personal boomboom, and that the writer is entitled to his boomboom: the satisfaction of pathological curiosity; a private bell for inexplicable needs; a bath; pecuniary difficulties; a stomach with repercussions in life; the authority of the mystic wand formulated as the bouquet of a phantom orchestra made up of silent fiddle bows greased with philtres made of chicken manure. With the blue eye-glasses of an angel they have excavated the inner life for a dime's worth of unanimous gratitude. If all of them are right and if all pills are Pink Pills, let us try for once not to be right. Some people think they can explain rationally, by thought, what they think. But that is extremely relative. Psychoanalysis is a dangerous disease, it puts to sleep the anti-objective impulses of men and systematizes the bourgeoisie.

There is no ultimate Truth. The dialectic is an amusing mechanism which guides us / in a banal kind of way / to the opinions we had in the first place. Does anyone think that, by a minute refinement of logic, he has demonstrated the truth and established the correctness of these opinions? Logic imprisoned by the senses is an organic disease. To this element philosophers always like to add: the power of observation. But actually this magnificent quality of the mind is the proof of its impotence. We observe, we regard from one or more points of view, we choose them among the millions that exist. Experience is also a product of chance and individual faculties. Science disgusts me as soon as it becomes a speculative system, loses its character of utility-that is so useless but is at least individual.

I detest greasy objectivity, and harmony, the science that finds everything in order. Carry on, my children, humanity . . . Science says we are the servants of nature: everything is in order, make love and bash your brains in. Carry on, my children, humanity, kind bourgeois and journalist virgins . . . I am against systems, the most acceptable system is on principle to have none. To complete oneself, to perfect oneself in one's own littleness, to fill the vessel with one's individuality, to have the courage to fight for and against thought, the mystery of bread, the sudden burst of an infernal propeller into economic lilies....

Every product of disgust capable of becoming a negation of the family is Dada; a protest with the fists of its whole being engaged in destructive action: Dada; knowledge of all the means rejected up until now by the shamefaced sex of comfortable compromise and good manners: Dada; abolition of logic, which is the dance of those impotent to create: Dada; of every social hierarchy and equation set up for the sake of values by our valets: Dada; every object, all objects, sentiments, obscurities, apparitions and the precise clash of parallel lines are weapons for the fight: Dada; abolition of memory: Dada; abolition of archaeology: Dada; abolition of prophets: Dada; abolition of the future: Dada; absolute and unquestionable faith in every god that is the immediate product of spontaneity: Dada; elegant and unprejudiced leap from a harmony to the other sphere; trajectory of a word tossed like a screeching phonograph record; to respect all individuals in their folly of the moment: whether it be serious, fearful, timid, ardent, vigorous, determined, enthusiastic; to divest one's church of *every useless cumbersome accessory; to spit out disagreeable or amorous ideas like a luminous waterfall, or coddle them -with the extreme satisfaction that it doesn't matter in the least-with the same intensity in the thicket of one's soul-pure of insects for blood well-born, and gilded with bodies of archangels. Freedom: Dada Dada Dada, a roaring of tense colours, and interlacing of opposites and of all contradictions, grotesques, inconsistencies: LIFE**

"I couldn't say I got any of the proceedings especially the horse headed girls.

6

Now and again you have to go with the flow, and before we knew it Blair went the way of Thatcher - he'd served his time - and in almost a copycat scenario, where Thatcher had been replaced by Major, Blair was replaced by Brown, another fucking duffer, who gulped for air as if he were swimming the hundred meter crawl. "Cuuu." A completely ineffectual asshole who couldn't have run a minodge. He did set up an inquiry into the reasons for Britain's involvement in the Iraq war - The Iraq Inquiry as it was known. That was a load of flam. The report when it came was a crushing verdict. Damning and scathing in equal measure. A crushing indictment of how Tony Blair rode roughshod over his cabinet. He lied.

"You know it's the blind leading the blind," said Joyce, as we dressed to go visit her mum, who hadn't been keeping well and needed cheering up. "Sometimes I wonder we ever get anywhere with the leaders we have. That's politics I suppose. You don't always get what you want."

"Never."

We went via Tesco to pick up milk. Chocolate biscuits, and cake.

Soon after the death of Ron, Joyce brought it to my attention she was worried about her mother's health. Nothing she could pin down to specifics she'd said. A weird feeling. The same feeling she'd had as a child before her father died; And she was concerned. That concerned we'd taken to calling in on her once a week. And that had been the case for the past six month. Always Saturday mornings.

"Hello mum. It's me," shouted Joyce, as I closed the door at our backs.

She was sitting in the living room watching tv, smoking a cigarette.

We both went in then gave her a kiss, asked her how she'd been.

"Fine," she said. Then I left the room to go make tea, whilst Joyce ran over the plans.

We were off in two days time for a three week trip to France. Nothing fancy, the bike and a tent. We'd made up our minds to explore the north west of the country, and while we were at it catch up with David and Rosa. It had been a while since we'd seen them, and we both agreed that as we'd be in their location it would only be right to visit. We'd take the bike down the west coast of England, stopping off at The Lakes then on to Blackpool, cut across country to Hull then the ferry across to Zeebrugge. From there we'd take our time and slowly make our way to Lannion.

First, we'd have to get arrangements right for Val's stay with Janine.

"Everything's packed and your ready to lift your stuff and go when the time comes?" I heard Joyce say, as I walked in carrying the tea.

I laid it on the table, filled three cups. Poured in milk then added sugar, passed them out to the girls.

"Janine'll be here tomorrow morning to pick you up at ten."

"I know," she said. "Everything's ready. Enjoy yourselves. I'll be fine staying with Janine. I won't be on my own. You'll be home before you know it. I'll see the two of you then."

Fine.

It was good she felt at ease staying with Janine. We didn't like to think of her being on her own - though she lived on her own. We were only four mile away, and popping in once a week as we'd now grown accustomed to doing always eased our minds. And if she needed us to fetch for her, or wasn't feeling too good, we were only a phone call away. Five minutes on the bike down the road if she felt the need. Janine was still in the borders area, sixty-nine mile away; Help in a sudden emergency strictly out of the question. It eased our minds when she said she'd go to Janine's while we were away.

Mum was always fine with Janine, it was Joyce had the problem there. With mum she couldn't do anything wrong, with Joyce she could do no right, and always went out of her way … Always had a spanner at hand.

Once we returned, we'd sort things out and mum would move in with us. We'd already broached the matter with her, tentatively, as knowing how much she loved her own home it wasn't an easy subject. We were confident, that once we pointed out the benefits, on our return, she'd finally brighten to the idea, and see it for what it was; A move for her future security and health. A family member on call. Until then, best if she kept it to herself till the details were ironed out. That way if there happened to be any hiccups Janine couldn't revel in gloat. "See, told you nothing would come of it. A pipe dream. What made you so sure mum would pack up and move in with you? Rather go into an old people's home than backtrack to that shithole you live in."

We'd sort it out the day of our return to minimise the flack.

With sick lines in we loaded up, then made our way down south.

First stop at the lakes was Dove Cottage and once inside I couldn't help notice how large it was. I don't know why I always imagined it smaller than it was. Poets on laudanum and wine. 'The school of whining and hypochondriacal poets that haunt the lakes.' Wordsworth, Coleridge and Southey.

"It's people like us," I said to Joyce, "that destroyed this place."

"The house, you mean, how come?"

"No not the house in particular. The area. The Lakes. People perceived it a certain way after reading their poetry and turned up in droves, and that was the end of that. The tranquillity was gone. The place lost its serenity and never recovered. It became a hotspot for tourism. Look at the crowd as we drove through Keswick, and it's like that everyday. Packed."

"I wouldn't live here," said Joyce. "I couldn't. Like you say, it is quite busy. People moving around like ants. Fuck that."

We didn't stay long once we'd seen the cottage, we headed straight for the Pool.

Blackpool was a different prospect all the same. You expected it to be crawling. Surface grime and peeling paint, the smell of fish and chips. And we were only there for The Pleasure Beach, down to ride the rides.

We parked the bike at the North Pier end then walked the Golden Mile.

"It's hard to believe you've only been here that once with auntie Sargent," I said. "Even as a child."

"It wasn't a place the family frequented. We always took the camper van and headed for the continent. Didn't matter where so long as we could park up and were left to get on with it. We particularly enjoyed Saint-Malo in France. They were good times. It didn't bother me I had to spend weeks in close proximity to Janine either. We mucked in and got on with it."

I laughed.

"This is Blackpool," I said, with feeling, joyful glee in my voice."

"I know," she said, as she looked at the place. "It is pretty grubby now."

"That's part of its charm," I said, as we stood and looked at the tower.

"It's Blackpool and that's what you get; Stag nights and hen parties, candyfloss and rock. The place is a riot at night with people staggering drunk. Kiss me quick hats and police helmets. Blow-up dolls and fancy dress. Half naked women and puke. Then during the day, you can't move for pushchairs and youngsters covered in ice cream and chocolate.

The place *is* a riot. That's what you love about it. It's Blackpool."

We continued along to the Central Pier then walked on out to its head.

"You know back in the day all the big names played Blackpool," I said. "The Beatles and Frank Sinatra. It was the place to be seen."

"Conceivable back in the day. Although it doesn't look like it's the place to be seen nowadays. Maybe the place not to be seen."

I laughed at that and then we played the slots. Went and got a hotdog each: onions, mustard, tomato sauce, a pale blue paper napkin. Proceeded along the Golden Mile, taking in the gift shops.

"Here," I said, "look at this," as I lifted a cock on a chain. "Never lose your keys with this in your bag."

"More like lose your sanity," said Joyce. "Do people actually by this shit, and if they do who are they?"

"Cock rock?"

Back on the promenade we could see The Big One in the distance - and as far as I was led to believe it was the tallest roller coaster in the world, or it was at the time of its construction. Once inside we joined the queue and awaited our turn to ride. One hour fifteen minutes later we sat our arses in a car.

We only managed four rides then it was time to leave. A tramcar back along to the bike, then eastward bound for Hull.

Ferry.

Once in Belgium we set up home in a campsite on the outskirts of Oudenburg to plan the journey ahead.

We spent a bit of time exploring the place, eating moules frites and waffles, then once we'd had a belly full, gassed-up the bike and left.

Ostend, Mariakerke, Raversijde-Bad, *Brrrm!*

We hugged the coast roads if we could and before we knew it arrived in De Panne where we visited the Adinkirke Military Cemetery to visit the grave of my parental grandfather who'd been killed on the Western Front during the First War and been laid to rest there. I had been there once before with my father when a child - the trip a haze. I couldn't remember much about it; rows of little headstones.

Then, eventually standing directly over it, we paid our respects then left. Crossed the border into France then made our way to the coast.

Ghyvelde, Leffrinckoucke, Rosendaël. Dunkirk, *Brrrm!*

The light was fading, the hour was getting late, and as the sun dipped slowly under the horizon, we pulled into Camping Du Casino, about twelve mile west of Dunkirk. This would afford us a break in the journey and let us take in the sights.

Next morning we were up before nine and made our way to Calais.

There was a restaurant there Joyce said I should try. "It's called Histoire Ancienne.

We used to frequent it when I came as a child. The escargot are nice. Mum loved them. We'd always stay a day or two in Calais as soon as we crossed the channel and when we did, this was our point of call. I love the place. It brings back memories."

Well …

For one believeth that he may eat
all things; another, who is weak, eateth
herbs.

let's go.

"Why not. We could visit the Lighthouse, then from there the art museum. By that time, we should be ready for lunch. What do you think, a plan?"

"A plan," she said. "Works for me. I for one will be starving."

And she was … And they were … Divine.

We were seated at a table for two and before I knew what was happening Joyce had ordered the nem d'escargots et petits légumes and the pigeonneau, which we shared and ate with gusto. This was followed by a dish of scallops and a small carafe of house wine. Forty minutes later we dived into lava cake, bursting to explode with rich, thick gooeyness. Espresso to finish off.

By the time we set out to leave the campsite we'd been on the road a week.

Our next destination was Perros-Guirec where we planned to walk the coast, have a look at one or two churches whilst there, and the statue of Saint-Guirec on the beach, before we drove to Sentier des Douaniers to visit another lighthouse.

Shit, I felt like one of the Stevensons, and said as much to Joyce.

"We'll soon be able to build these things if we visit any more of them. I'll have the hang of it by then. What do you think; change my name to Stevenson?"

She looked at me with that blank expression that said it all. I could see she'd missed the point completely, so opted to cut it short.

"Lighthouses."

"Sometimes you're not on this planet … Robert, Alan, David or Thomas?"

Now who was looking blank? I walked right into that one and should have known better. If I was being a smart ass she threw it back in my face. She'd a knack … And knew how to use it in each situation … a seasoned comedian's pause.

We laughed as we strolled along hand-in-hand.

"Well, it wasn't Robert Louis."

"Much too dapper for that," I said.

*Say not of me that weakly I declined
The labours of my sires, and fled the sea,
The towers we founded and the lamps we lit,
To play at home with paper like a child.
But rather say: In the afternoon of time
A strenuous family dusted from its hands
The sand of granite, and beholding far
Along the sounding coast its pyramids
And tall memorials catch the dying sun,
Smiled well content, and to this childish task
Around the fire addressed its evening hours.* *

Camping Tourony was our last port of call before dropping in on David and Rosa. They knew we were on our way, so there wouldn't be any surprise. We'd called them, on reaching Calais, to inform them we were coming, and as such were expected. We could have made the journey straight from Sentier des Douaniers, after viewing the lighthouse, but as there was a pressing need to take care of laundry as soon as possible - rather than commandeer David and Rosa's facilities, in the event they were overrun with guests - we went with a stay at the campsite. Plus, it allowed us time to relax and take in the coastline before we got to them. Time out to catch our breath and unwind. Lie about in the sun.

And we did.

Three days of doing nothing except eat and drink, looking at the stars overhead at night, and cooking up a storm on the Coleman. Nice. Sausage, ham and eggs and beans. One pot stew and soup. We were loathed to leave when we finally did but time was running out.

David and Rosa's for our last few days then that would see us homeward bound. Back to work and the old routine. Get Val settled in. That was the one thing Joyce couldn't wait for, to get Val settled in.

"I can see the look on Janine's face now, when we tell her … I can't wait … Can you imagine it? That smug look she carries on her face will be wiped away forever. Game set and match to Joyce. She lifts the cup overhead."

I could tell by her demeaner she couldn't wait; it was obvious. And I suspected that if we hadn't been surrounded with fellow campers, likewise taking the sun, she may have danced in her pants, then rolled in the sand. "Yeeha!" Finally at one with her environment. Happy at last to have won the match with the very last kick of the ball.

I could wait till we got mum home then popped a bottle of champagne. POP!

David and Rosa were glad to see us and made us feel at home.

Four days later we said our goodbyes and climbed aboard the bike. *Brrrm!*

7

We returned a week later than either of us planned to the spiteful doings of Janine.
 Then landmine went off with devastating effect, its intended target rocked.

"What do you mean dead?" screamed Joyce, as she steadied herself from the blast.
 "Exactly what I said," replied Janine. "Died the morning you left."
 Joyce stood straight, her hand on a chair, then spat right back in her face.
 "I always knew you were scum, Janine, but even for you … You're sick … Where the hell is she?"
 She brushed past her sister then made for the living room, pushed the door open wide.
 "Where the hell is she Janine." It was empty; except for a cat on the couch.
 "For all the things you could possibly have said, that was the lowest of the low. Now, for the last time … where is she?"
 I suspected the supermarket or visiting her friend Nanette, myself, as she had recourse to call in on her to see how she was keeping, as a lump on her left breast had been diagnosed as cancerous and she was now undergoing a course of chemotherapy in a concerted attempt to halt its spread.

going home
amen
show me the place
darkness.

anyhow / coming out
banjo
different side.

She had to have been somewhere, and at this juncture I suspected upstairs taking a nap, or out back weeding the garden. I opted for the later, as she loved a spot of gardening. I walked to the window and looked out back. Nothing but grass and plants.

"For the last time," Janine, "where is she? Enough of your fucking shite."

"Like I told you, she's dead. If you want me to, I'll go fetch her, then you can see for yourself."

She left the room and we then heard footsteps making their way upstairs.

"Exactly as I suspected," said Joyce. "Upstairs taking a nap." And as that was my initial impression, I assumed it more than likely.

"Most likely," I said. I wasn't for leaving. Not now. I was seeing this through to the end. Things were about to get interesting, and I didn't want to miss out. Usually, I left when the two of them got at it. This was different. Hell no. I was staying. I wasn't about to miss this.

Janine returned with a wooden ashes casket and handed it to Joyce.

Well … as far as I could see the place was about to erupt and I wasn't far off the mark.

"What the fuck is this?" screamed Joyce, as she took the wooden box.

"Mum," said Janine. "I told you she was dead. Dead and cremated as well. Died the day you left. I told you … Massive heart attack."

Joyce looked down at the shiny brass plaque and didn't believe her eyes.

"This is the limit, Janine. Of all the stunts you've pulled in your time, this has got to be up there. You're a fucking scumbag, and not funny at all. It's one big joke to you. Now where the fucking hell is she?"

"Are you thick, Joyce?" she said. "Read the fucking lid."

Joyce looked down at the inscription on the plaque, and slowly read what it said:

In Memory of
Valerie Arnold
1. 7. 1931 – 14. 8. 2009
Until We Meet Again, I Will Love You For Ever

She froze on the spot, then let the thing drop. It went off like a megaton nuclear bomb, in the deafening stillness of the room. It bounced itself into six separate pieces that spun, slow motion, in the air. Her ashes came down in their plastic bag and hit the floor like a dump. PLUMP!

You've only got yourself to blame," said Janine. "If you had bought a mobile phone when I told you to do so you wouldn't be in this situation. I'd have been able to contact you wherever you were. No, that's the last thing you're about to do: take advice from your sister."

An eerie silence then prevailed, which lasted forever and a day.

Joyce attacked.

SLAP!

"Sister? Don't call yourself my sister. You're a caustic bitch. Who in their right mind pulls a stunt like this and thinks it's funny?"

"I didn't exactly think it was funny. What gave you that idea?"

"Whatever you can do to upset me and get yourself a laugh into the bargain, that's what gave me that idea. So long as the laugh's at my expense, that's alright by you. You're a bitch Janine, and you know it."

"You're not right in the head. You're always putting blame on me. Does it not strike you as funny or slightly odd that every time a situation arises where your life isn't going quite to plan, and I'm involved, it's always down to me? Does that not strike you as strange? It was down to logistics, Joyce. She was dead and had to be cremated. We couldn't wait for you to return, when we didn't know where you were."

"Nothing strange about it. It's always down to you. You're a fucking nightmare on legs Janine. A fucking nightmare on legs."

She turned as if to make for the door and Janine pulled her back with a …

"You forgot what you came for, Joyce. Don't leave empty handed. Take her with you. It's what you came for, is it not; to have her move in with you when you got back from the continent ..? Well, there she is, lying on the floor. Pick her up and take her."

I could see in Joyce's face she was stunned. How did she know about that? She'd told mum not to say a word; to wait till we got back.

"How did you know about that?" she asked, determined to get to the bottom.

"Easy enough," said Janine, with a grin and sudden lift of her brow. "Mother told me weeks ago of your plan. Did you think she'd have kept that from me? I don't think so. And I don't think she was comfortable with the prospect of it either, going by what she told me."

I could tell she was about to strike again, that last remark cutting deep. I grabbed her by the arm before she struck and turned her toward the door. I bent and lifted the ashes from the floor, and in seconds we were out on the drive.

"Get in," I said, "she's not worth the bother. Don't give her the satisfaction, she'll only revel in its glow, you know what she's like. A calculating cow."

I straddled the bike then kicked it to life.

Next again day we picked up an urn from a funeral parlour in the city. Popped in Val, gave it a polish, then sat it on the mantle next to gran.

8

We'd only got over the death of mother when another shock hit.

Gordon Brown, the useless fucking arsehole that had been running the country for the last two and a half year, had asked the Queen for permission to dissolve parliament on 12 April, ensuring a general election date of 6 May 2010. And all going well I had made up my mind to vote nationalist in the hope we'd once and for all escape the English yoke and, over time, manage to gain independence, and thus ensure our destiny lay in our own hands. Who was I kidding? Once again, the Tories gained control, though it wasn't all plain sailing. Although they won with the most votes and seats, they ultimately fell twenty seats short to command a majority in the House of Commons which resulted in a hung parliament. There'd need to be a coalition. Labour put up an abortive attempt to side with the Liberal Democrats and gain support from a number of smaller parties to make up the shortfall, then ultimately the Liberal Democrats, in their great wisdom, sided with the Tories, forcing Brown to resign next day and sidle off to his lair. We ended up with Cameron/Clegg; what a fucking double act that was.

"A waste of time," I said to Joyce. "I don't know why I bother."

"What?"

"Aligning myself with the nationalist cause when it doesn't make a difference. As far as I can see I'm wasting my vote. I'd be better not bothering. Back to the way I was. That'd be the best thing for me."

"Wait … You only think your vote's a waste of time; it's not an overnight process. Look what happened in 2007 when the SNP staged a historic upset by putting an end to fifty years of Labour dominance in the Scottish Parliament elections. If we keep a hold on things up here the way we're doing for now, you never know, the powers that be in Westminster may determine a referendum on Scottish independence the right way to go. That will only happen if we keep the majority here. If we let that slide, we're doomed. Doomed to be under the English yoke for the foreseeable future. Not a prospect worth thinking about. All we can do is knuckle down and see what the future brings."

I dunked a digestive into my tea, where it broke and fell in the cup.

"That always happens," I said, digging out what I could with the bowl of a spoon then sucking it off the end. "Do you think a chocolate digestive has better structural integrity than an ordinary one?"

She looked at me before she replied, wheels going round in her head. "Oat biscuits are best," she said, "as far as I'm led to believe. They've got a low absorbency rate and a high dunk break point. Thirty seconds tops at a guess … Possibly thirty five."

"Wow … What's the news on the Janine front?" I asked, before she moved to crackers.

"What do you mean?"

"Val's house and possessions. What's happening with them? Does she get the lot?"

"She's welcome to them. She can keep her blood money."

"It's hardly blood money, now is it?"

"It's Blood money, and it doesn't matter how you dress it up, Jeff, don't kid yourself. It's money obtained at the cost of another's life. And for all we know, the bitch might have killed her."

"That's a bit strong. Whatever she is she's not a murderer."

"I wouldn't put it past her. She's capable of anything if it gets at me."

"Murder? That's a bit on the strong side."

"I wouldn't put it past her, that's all I'm saying. The bastard can rot in hell."

I left it at that, in the knowledge that to carry on would be futile. It'd be like banging my head against a brick wall, and whatever I said would be meaningless. When it came to Janine, in Joyce's mind, the verdict had already been returned; Guilty. Guilty as charged, with no appeal. Throw away the key.

At the end of November, we received an invite from Miriam and Eunice to attend a Hogmanay ceilidh in their local town hall. And ceilidhs being ceilidhs, any idea of declining never entered our heads. Plus, it was a thing to look forward to; A good old knees-up was what was needed to lift the mood, and put a smile on Joyce's face, after Janine's shenanigans.

We RSVP'd next day for fear of missing out. Because we knew, as with all such occasions, there'd only be limited capacity, and if you weren't in as soon as the tickets went on sale you were likely to miss out. And missing out on letting the hair down we weren't prepared to do.

"You'll be wearing a kilt of course?" said Joyce. I knew she was at the jest.

She was well aware of my feelings concerning that stereotypical piece of garb and might as well have enquired as to whether or not I'd be wearing a Jimmy wig.

"Not even if you were wearing a short cutty sark and were dancing a jig like Nannie."

"Ha … You should be so lucky," she said. "Easier win the lottery."

"I should be so lucky. Lucky, lucky, lucky." One for the blue stone man.

First things first.

The bike had been playing up recently, and I suspected it was on its last legs. No harm to it. It had served us well, and when we pushed it to its limit it complied without complaint. So long as you oiled it now and again and filled it's belly with gas, it didn't ask for much. Now it had reached its pensionable age I reluctantly stored it away. I Put it in the garage then covered it up. Gave it a pat, then left.

We scoured the ads in What Car? mag before making up our minds.

We opted for a wee Fiat 500, as much like the bike, we were both pushing on ourselves. We weren't in our thirties or forties any longer and our days of getting swept with wind and rain, when the weather turned, would need to become a thing of the past. We liked to travel in comfort these days. Our bones were beginning to creak.

It was a tiny red number with dents and dinks and ran like a clockwork toy.

Then all of a sudden it was Christmas again which with the passing of years arrived with speed and a frightening regularity.

We sat on the couch watching telly and stuffing our faces with crap.

ceilidh

A cèilidh (KAY-lee, Scottish Gaelic: [ˈkʲʰeːlɪ]) or céilí (Irish: [ˈceːlʲiː]) is a traditional Scottish or Irish social gathering. In its most basic form, it means a social visit. In contemporary usage, it usually involves dancing and playing Gaelic folk music, either at a house party or a larger concert at a social hall or other community gathering place. Cèilidhean (plural of cèilidh) and céilithe (plural of céilí) originated in the Gaelic areas of Scotland and Ireland and are consequently common in the Scottish and Irish diasporas. They are similar to the Troyl traditions in Cornwall and Twmpath and Noson Lawen events in Wales, as well as English country dances throughout England which have in particular areas undergone a fusion with céilithe.

The morning after the event I was done. The realisation I wasn't as young as I was, was slowly dawning, and my body was getting the message. It told me; Ellis, you're not twenty now. You're not even thirty or forty. And I knew it was right. I knew it was time I started acting my age instead of thinking I could party like I used to without there being any ... "How rough do I feel? I think I'm about to die." I needed Alka Seltzer and quick, along with a cup of coffee.

Eunice obliged with a plink, plink, fizz, then laid the glass in front of me. Made me a coffee with sugar and milk in the largest mug I'd seen.

Miriam cooked scrambled egg and toast and a beautiful fried tomato.

After that, I must admit, I felt better. The decision to remain another day had been made and I was glad it had. The drive back north was not a prospect that filled me with joy, the way I was feeling. I wasn't hungover or anything; I was completely wiped. I didn't suffer from the usual hangover symptoms, like headaches. With me it was always a dodgy gut until I got two Alka Seltzers down and then I felt whacked. A lethargy that rose from the soles of my feet then spread up through to my head. Lying on the couch was as much as I could manage on days such as this. And Miriam and Eunice being who they were obliged my post drunk indulgence.

I felt like a king, and if trophies were ever to be handed out for the art of pamper then Miriam and Eunice would get CHAMPS. They brought me a cover, the remote control for the television set, crisps, and nuts, and chocolate.

"Lemon chicken alright for dinner?" asked Eunice as she tucked me in.

"For heaven's sake," said Joyce, from the kitchen, "you won't get the bugger to leave. He's not used to that sort of treatment you know. And if he thinks

I'm carrying on where you two leave off, when we get home, he's another think coming."

I knew I'd have to make best of a good thing, so asked for a glass of milk.

Miriam brought in a strawberry shake, with cream and a cherry on top.

As I lay there feeding my face with goodies, the idea of the lemon chicken for dinner was making me salivate.

9

Once home, I read.
    I had returned to The Heart Sutra at the end of November in the hope of gaining a grip, and each time I was sure I was making headway it ran away from me again. I was always on the cusp of a great understanding only to be bit on the ass. I was having difficulty figuring out the whole emptiness thing. That escaped me and remained elusive. I couldn't find this in that and that's what was troubling me. I was searching for this in that, and the longer I searched the further from my grasp it got. It could be it required my undivided attention, or else I was paying it too much, and trying too hard to find things that weren't there. Or, as I truly suspected when Joyce first tried to explain it to me, it was gibberish. Foreign nonsense from the hippy era. A remnant of days gone by. Hairy-fairy stardust.
    One thing was for sure; It had me in its grip, and I wasn't for giving up.

Who in the world eats margarine?
Who in the world eats oil?
Give me lard and butter.
Foods to fry not broil.

Sugar by the bucket load;
make me feel quite queer.

Things to block my arteries,
vodka, gin, and beer.

We gained the majority in the Scottish Parliament in the 2011 vote, and at last I felt my **X** for the SNP had counted, rather than being the wasted vote I felt it had been in the past. This was our opportunity, and all going well - the Independence Movement keeping up the surge - I felt the breakaway was in sight, and that within five or six year we could become a fully autonomous country, with all the benefits that entailed, and to be able to say, we're free. Hold our heads up high at last, a sovereign nation again

  Sixty-nine seats out of a total of a hundred and twenty-nine. Our nearest rival Labour.

Come, Avalanche, take me with you when you fall! *

We sold the bike when an offer we couldn't refuse came in and put the money in the pot. We'd built a substantial nest egg - or so we believed - as a buffer against our creeping old age and decrepitude. It wasn't that it was on our minds in any troubling way, it's only we'd discussed the matter and come to an agreement that anything was better than nothing. The state pension - and ever grateful to that particular benefit - would only allow us to survive, forever treading water. It was all very well being mortgage free, but by the time we laid-out for gas, electricity, and food, whatever luxuries we intended purchasing would remain luxuries. And by the looks of things, by the time we reached retirement age, luxuries would include toilet roll.

I threw shopping bags in the back of the car. Returned to the house to pick up the shopping list Joyce was compiling at the table.

The weathermen told us today we'd have sun, so we were going to barbie.

"Now," she said, as I lifted the list. "Cheese slices … Don't get cheesy."

"What's the difference?" I asked.

"Cheese is real, that's all. Cheesy's full of emulsifiers and all sorts of other shit. And low fat beef mince. Don't get frozen, hell knows what's in that."

Instructions uploaded into the computer I made for the thrill of the mall.

And it was a thrill.

I was a sucker for packaging and as I walked the aisles all sorts caught my eye, then before I knew it the trolley I was pushing was filled to overflowing. I was enamoured by tins of sardines from Portugal. La Rose and Santo Amaro. Bottles of Spanish olive oil. Vigo and Nuñez De Prado. Colourful Italian pasta packaging. Ox & Palm, corned beef. Myriad brands of hot sauce.

I could have spent the day going up and down and struggled to pull myself away, only I knew the sun was calling

"Fucking hell Jeff. We already have umpteen tins of sardines," said Joyce on my return.

"I know," I replied, "These are for the cellar. You can't have too much. I also got us butterbeans.

Treacle and a tin of golden syrup. Salt and a curry mix."

"Did you get beef mince?

I said I did. "And cheese instead of cheesy."

I washed my hands then set to the task of preparing the food for our broil.

Joyce lit the barbeque using a rapid fire chimney loaded with lumpwood charcoal.

"Don't put onion or chilli in the burgers."

"No." I never did.

I always liked to keep them as plain as possible and never went for the quarter pounder, always opting to make them as thin as I could, only adding salt and pepper. If you wished to add chillies and any other filler, then you were quite at liberty to do so after it was on the bun. Your choice. There was an array of condiments and salad to choose from.

Joyce ran a cable from the garage to the pergola, plugged in a small radio.

We were good to go, and anyone turning up would have drawn the conclusion there were more people on the premises than Joyce and myself, by the amount of food that was on the table, and wondered where they were. We were set and aimed to make a day of it. The sun was out and there wasn't a cloud in the sky, and as this was a rare occasion it'd be a shame to pass it up. We were here for the long haul and the table said it all.

Soy sauce, tomato sauce, brown sauce, Sriracha. Four bottles of Spanish wine: two red, two white, a dozen cans of beer. Pickles and chillies, a sourdough loaf. Butter and mustards and Jam. Salad cream, mayonnaise, a tin of Royal Dansk.

Cooked burgers, sausages and lamb chops, corn on the cob and asparagus. Cheese slices, bitter chocolate. 85%.

We had a charcuterie board under a net cloche - an homage to gran - and a large bowl of salad. Jugs of water, lemonade, orange juice, and gin.

"If we could depend on the weather, Ellis, we wouldn't go abroad."

"I don't suppose we would. The problem with that is if we did have the weather then we wouldn't have the beauty. Can you imagine our white-sand beaches built up like the resorts in Spain and other countries where they do get the weather? Some of those resorts where nothing more than fishing villages till the dollar-kick took hold. Now they're unrecognizable. Would you rather have that or the pristine coastline we have, rain and wind thrown in?"

"Mmm. Built-up chaotic holiday resorts or unspoiled silver sands? Dick."

She reached for a sausage then put it on a bun, ketchup and yellow mustard.

"How about this one … If you could meet anyone, who would it be?"

That was easy.

"No one," I answered. "Most people in the public eye are fucks and are up their own arses. You know what they say, never meet your heroes. That's true. Those in the arts are playing a part and you don't want to take off the mask. Same thing with politicians, only they're a bunch of liars. They lie for a living, and hell mend us if any of them told the truth. It's second nature to them, lying. They've been at it that long they can't tell the difference. And when all's said and done, they're exactly the same as us. They all shit and piss in the toilet every day and sit in their pants eating pizza."

She laughed at this and said I was right. "Keith and Mick in their pants and socks, sitting on a couch eating pizza."

"Shit," I said. "The mind boggles. Not an image I needed."

An Amazon driver delivered a parcel. We offered him food and drink.

Images of war profligate.
From birth till the present day
worldwide.
Constant and out of control.

They wish you to vote for the
Warmonger Devils.
Cunts
devoid of a soul.

Then the unthinkable happened: a phone call from Lena, informing us Jules had died and the news that David Cameron was to give the go ahead for the Scottish parliament to hold a referendum on Scottish independence.

Sadness tinged with joy.
We wept.
And then we danced till four.

Lena told us Jules dropped dead on a day trip to Cologne, and as she hadn't been with him, she never said goodbye, and that was the one thing that troubled her.

She'd accepted his death, as over the years they'd discussed the inevitable, and each had assured the other that when the time came and one of them passed away the other would carry on as before and, given the opportunity - under the right set of circumstances - hopefully marry again.

She couldn't get over the way he died and not having said goodbye. It was playing on her mind, and she couldn't sleep. The doctor had given her medication. She struggled. She didn't fancy being on tablets for the rest of her life, but for the time being it was the only way she could get an hour or two shut-eye. Vivid dreams then plagued her she said, visions of Jules and herself:

They came for the purpose of war not trade.
  "Spring the corpse of Hastein."
Trains were derailed,
ships went down.
  "Women and children first."

She didn't know what to make of them, she said. "I've sent you a poem in the mail."
  We waited.

Cameron bumped-off Gaddafi, in another dirty-not-our-war.
  Maybe it was guilt. Hard to say. I doubted it very much.
  "I don't know he had any choice other than go the way he went," said Joyce. "Not after the majority

gained in the Scottish parliament by the SNP at the last vote. Now that he has, he's backed himself into a corner. There are those within the Tory party and elsewhere that see his decision to support a referendum a reckless gamble … A risk … He knows the Scottish people have voted overwhelmingly for a party that wants independence and has granted our wish. If he ends up losing, and is then seen as the prime minister who was responsible for the break up of the Union, he'll have no option other than to resign."

"Has he given a date when the vote will be held, or is it all still nothing but fantasy?"

"I don't think it's fantasy. From what I read in the paper he was genuine enough. As for any dates forthcoming, nothing on that front yet."

"Mm."

A cardboard tube containing a painting: a composite of Thatcher and Blair. The first two quarter diagonals Thatcher. The second two quarters Blair.

It was vampire-like, and traces of blood could be seen on their teeth, their eyes a glaring red.

It was his weirdest painting to date, and we loved it. It was larger than the two we had, so we hung it on the opposite wall.

Dear Joyce/Jeffery

I hope this finds you well.

Please find enclosed the last painting completed by Jules before his untimely death.

Please accept it with my blessing, and all the love in the world.

Also enclosed is the poem I promised. Hope you enjoy.

Lena.

**He dared to dream
flowers and spicy sky bonbons.**

He took the bull by the horns
and ran the streets of Pamplona.
  The world was his oyster,
full of cliché,
he dined with angels and Blake.

He supped from the Loving Cup
wonderment and pleasure.
  The life of the extrovert,
always on show,
his tin gun loaded with ray.

A plane on a sun-cloud,
haloed as angel,
he lived it at night as in day.
His lightening flashed quickly,
his bolt burst his bubble,
a blink of an eye then away.
Lena.

*

BOOK FOUR

*

Resolving internal party disputes, Cameron may end up in a truss.

1

And he was true to his word. And the date was set. And we voted on 18 September 2014, marking our paper with our **X**.

The question was simple - 'Should Scotland be an independent country?' - and the one most favoured by the Electoral Commission out of the four possible versions they had.

Nonetheless, I was concerned. And said as much to Joyce.

"I'm not convinced we'll get the result we want. I reckon the Unionist's will carry the day. I can feel it in my bones. It'll be a close run thing. I think they'll take it in the end. They'll crawl out of the woodwork to keep the Union together, that's how staunch they are. And if they do, we can wave goodbye to any future vote for a while. It'll be a once in a generation thing, and only that if the SNP don't shoot themselves in the foot, which tends to be the case with political parties once they've been in power a certain amount of time. They end up crumbling and dragging the country down in a deep, dark hole."

"You've got to have faith Ellis. You can't be negative all the time, it doesn't do any good. If you think it's going to be a close run thing then it could go either way. We may get up on the nineteenth to discover we're independent … Faith, Ellis. That's all you need. A little faith."

They'd been living in relative comfort in a fertile river delta for five hundred years, raiding neighbours and city states, deep in the interior, when they felt the need for blood and precious metals. They were animals and proud of the fact, and the kudos bestowed upon them by their Elders on their return - heavily laden with gourds of slaughter, silver and bars of gold - was praise above and beyond.
 They were an insular people and the only time they ventured out was to pillage and rape. They did not welcome outsiders with any degree of acceptance. They openly discouraged their assimilation with threats of deportation and death. They took to the sea and turned pirate. They became slavers. Their Empire was larger than Rome's had been. They ruled a quarter of the globe.
 Their days were numbered, and they did not know.
 Abiding in the midst of ignorance, thinking themselves wise and learned, fools going aimlessly hither and thither, like blind that are led by the blind.

The girls made their appearance on the morning of the eighteenth, after having cast their vote the minute their polling station opened, Miriam with a two dozen case of lager, Eunice, four bottles of wine.

They'd called to enquire if we wouldn't mind their company for the result of the vote when it came in, expressing their wish - that if we did gain independence - to be in the best company possible, and being flattered they chose us, said yes.

"Where are the flags?" asked Eunice, as she lifted the bottles of wine from the boot.

"We don't have any," said Joyce. "We didn't think about that."

"Not to worry," said Miriam. "We've come prepared."

She reached in the rear and pulled out a bag with a massive Saltire inside.

"Never leave home without one," she said, then waved it about in the wind. It clacked.

"That should cover the couch," I said. "Anything else for the walls?"

"Two posters, a string of bunting, and a picture of fat boy Salmond."

We brunched on salami, cheese and rye bread, once we'd draped the flag. Played a round of Trivial Pursuit and then moved on to Monopoly.

Eight forty-five we ordered Indian, opened the wine, drank a few beers then turned on Scotland Decides.

We got fucked.

The final result was declared by the Counting Officer at nine the following morning. We already knew. The BBC had declared, 'Scotland votes no,' on screen hours before, and our spirits were decidedly low.

"Well, that's one Salmond that didn't make it upstream," I said, trying to lighten the mood. The humour was missed or deliberately ignored, or it could have been a victim of exhaustion.

The long range weather forecast now looked decidedly grim.

The colonies revolted. Thirteen in total. They'd had enough and couldn't take it any longer. They were being bled dry by the Empire and wished to be masters of their own destiny, and revolution was in the air.

Ode for General Washington's Birthday

No Spartan tube, no Attic shell,
  No lyre Æolian I awake;
'Tis liberty's bold note I swell,
  Thy harp, Columbia, let me take.
See gathering thousands, while I sing,
A broken chain, exulting, bring,
  And dash it in a tyrant's face!
And dare him to his very beard,
And tell him he no more is fear'd
  No more the despot of Columbia's race.
A tyrant's proudest insults brav'd,
They shout, a People freed! They hail an Empire saved.

  Where is man's godlike form?
  Where is that brow erect and bold,
  That eye that can, unmov'd, behold
  The wildest rage, the loudest storm,
That e'er created fury dared to raise!
  Avaunt! thou caitiff, servile, base,

That tremblest at a despot's nod,
  Yet, crouching under the iron rod,
Canst laud the hand that struck th' insulting blow!
  Art thou of man's Imperial line?
  Dost boast that countenance divine?
  Each skulking feature answers, No!
  But come, ye sons of Liberty,
  Columbia's offspring, brave as free,
In danger's hour still flaming in the van,
Ye know, and dare maintain, the Royalty of Man.

  Alfred! on thy starry throne
  Surrounded by the tuneful choir,
The bards that erst have struck the patriot lyre,
And rous'd the freeborn Briton's soul of fire,
  No more thy England own. -
Dare injured nations form the great design,
  To make detested tyrants bleed?
Thy England execrates the glorious deed!
  Beneath her hostile banners waving,
  Every pang of honour braving,
  England in thunder calls - "The tyrant's cause is mine!"
  That hour accurst, how did the fiends rejoice,
And hell, thro' all her confines raise th' exulting voice,
  That hour which saw the generous English name Linkt with such damned deeds of everlasting shame!

Thee, Caledonia, thy wild heaths among,
Fam'd for the martial deed, the heaven-taught song,

To thee, I turn with swimming eyes. -
Where is that soul of Freedom fled?
Immingled with the mighty Dead!
Beneath that hallow'd turf where WALLACE lies!
Hear it not, Wallace, in thy bed of death!
Ye babbling winds in silence sweep;
Disturb not ye the hero's sleep,
Nor give the coward secret breath. -
Is this the ancient Caledonian form,
Firm as the rock, resistless as the storm?
Shew me that eye which shot immortal hate,
Blasting the despot's proudest bearing:
Shew me that arm which, nerv'd with thundering fate,
Braved Usurpation's boldest daring!
Dark-quench'd as yonder sinking star,
No more that glance lightens afar;
That palsied arm no more whirls on the waste of war. -*

They sparred again in the war of 1812, then indirectly, during the period they were fighting among themselves, supplying the CSA with all manner of goods, from luxury items to weapons, shipped across the Atlantic by blockade runners, mostly funded by those with private interests.

Hail to the Chief, my arse.

"I'm finished," I said to Joyce.

"What do you mean by that?"

"The entire independence thing and voting SNP. In fact, voting in general. It's a load of bullshit. At the end of the day politicians are only in it for what they can get; Independence or not. They'll end up like the rest of the fuckers; in too long then implode. It's inevitable. Once they're in power for ten or twelve years, corruption and stagnation sets in. Then you get party infighting and scandal. Sexual indiscretion and fraud. It's unavoidable. Comes with the territory. Wait and see. Ten or fifteen year down the line, if the SNP are still in power in Scotland, they'll shoot themselves in the foot."

Joyce made coffee then finally spoke. "You still have to utilize your vote."

"Forever the idealist," I said.

She shot back then laughed, "Fuck you."

They had a Great War. The naming of which was totally inappropriate as there was nothing remotely great about it. On the contrary, the whole thing was a shit-show, up to their knees in mud and blood, dysentery and trench foot. Home in time for turkey and pud, job done and dusted? The Empire rules the world.

They got turkey and pud alright; Gallipoli and smooth bore muzzle loading plum pudding. Ferried off to Mesopotamia, Ypres, Verdun or the Somme.

The Colonies joining the struggle when the Lusitania was sunk by a U-boat and a threatened alliance between Germany and Mexico against them reached their ears. Better late than never.

By the end of it The Empire was in hock to the people they once held sway over. Still a mighty power in itself, it's social structure slightly flattened. Nothing to worry about here folks, The Empire rules the world.

Cameron gets in for a second term. Clegg resigns as his party is routed.

We filled the car and headed for the North Coast 500 shortly after its inception, of the mind it was about time to take the plunge and see parts of the country completely alien. Beautiful. And on our return never let up talking about it for weeks, to any one who'd listen.

Man in the Post Office, blah, blah, blah.

Woman in the bank, blah.

They'd see us coming and rush for the exit. People being trampled underfoot.

"Here come the spouters of mental weariness. Every man for himself."

"It's time we stopped going on about our road trip," I said to Joyce. "People are beginning to get bored."

"I was thinking about that myself," she said. "Do you think we may be getting boring?"

"Old?"

"Don't say that," she said, offended. "I'd hate to think I was getting old. Boring's bad enough. Old's ten times worse."

"Old and boring, how about that? Soon to be deceased."

"Perhaps our decision not to have children has come back to haunt us. If we'd had children when we discussed it, there's a chance there'd be grandchildren by now. Always good for staving off the years."

"More commodities? ... We made the correct decision when we decided against it. Look at the life we've had. That wouldn't have been possible if there had been children. Not the way we played it."

"I know you're right. It has been fun. Now and again I wonder what it would have been like all the same. Don't you?"

"Never."

After the second global conflict The Empire disintegrated, and a new world order sprung up. The colonies, now consolidated into one United States with the power to destroy the planet, had become the dominant force. The Empire had become subservient, and whenever The States said jump they jumped, through hoops of burning fire.

A Cold War followed between these United States and the Soviet Union, the Western and Eastern Blocs.

The Empire's sphere of influence - much in evidence for well over three hundred years - was much diminished and rapidly declining.

They joined forces with a European Union in a new attempt to achieve economic growth and military security. They wished to integrate themselves but weren't fully committed. They were arrogant.

The single currency was not to their taste, they had the pound, and it was theirs.

"Your Empire gone johnny. Pull in your neck. Your whipping post holds no fear."

2

bchfyr: A holding term.

Operations continued as before, and if we could contact Greta Garbo all well and good. If not, we'd burn in hell.

It happened under dark of night, and as we thundered along at a rate of knots completely unknown to your everyday individual the extravagance and intrigue it generated was proportional to that first gulp of air of a newborn.

Comfort and luxury led the way. It was an addiction.

Agatha Christie would have been impressed by the sheer volume of murders. Nancy, Stuttgart, Munich, Vienna. Budapest, Belgrade, Nis.

"Ask the creator," screamed Vaslav, from the window. "This is high society."

He drew his head back in the nick of time, the up train whistling by.

"Close as I like it to get," he said. A splash of eau de cologne.

"It's either concealed in a diplomatic bag, or that baby grand piano. If the latter's the case, we may be undone. That bird's already flown. It's disappeared into thin air. That's the Americans for you."

His wife shovelled in her chicken chasseur, washed down with French champagne.

She dug a spoon into a souffle. "It isn't in here," she said.

Vaslav drew her a look of anger, puffed on the end of his cigar.

"If you don't have anything constructive to say, best say nothing at all."

Diplomacy was something he'd learned in the Corp then carried into everyday life.

They entered a tunnel. The lights grew dim. His wife shot out the door.

The operation was drawing to an end, Szilveszter Matuska on the line.

The never did find Greta Garbo.

3

"I don't believe it," I said to Joyce. "Have you seen the news? Cameron's set a date for the referendum to leave the European Union. He's briefed the cabinet and announced the date as 23 June. He's for staying, though his long-time ally Gove's aligned himself with the leave campaign. And as for the commons leader, Grayling; he believes the EU is holding the country back. He doesn't think we can take decisions in the national interest so long as we're a member.

What do you think?"

"Mm?"

She was fresh from bed and sat beside me in her dressing gown, jammies and drool.

"Cameron. He's set the date for the EU referendum."

She lifted a piece of cold, buttered toast, then nibbled a corner.

"What?"

"Cameron," I said. "He's set the date for the EU referendum."

"Taking a chance there," she said. "It'll be a close run thing. He's only trying to appease the sceptics in parliament along with the grassroot members who haven't seen being a part of the union as a positive thing. Most of them don't have a good word to say about it, along with the Tory press. It's all been negative from the start. They'll never be happy with anything they don't have a hundred per cent control over. They're still irked about their Empire."

"Yea, it's about time they gave that ghost up. I agree. My feeling is that if Cameron loses this one, all hell will break loose. Not necessarily in the short-term. The effects will take time to filter through - after a long, drawn out fight at the negotiating table - then once they do, a lot of people who voted leave will be wishing they voted remain. I foresee a collapse in the economy."

"The leavers are still of an imperialist mindset." said Joyce. "Once we've been dragged out and the country starts to nosedive into recession, they'll blame others. They're not the type to take responsibility for there actions. It'll be the European Commission or some other body's responsibility for the terms and conditions imposed in the withdrawal agreement. They won't hold their hands up and say they got it wrong. It's not in their DNA. They'd rather walk the plank."

4

They got themselves a bus.

We send the EU £350 million a week
let's fund our NHS instead
Let's take back control   Vote leave

"Have you ever seen such nonsense?" said Joyce. "And there he is, waving a Cornish pasty about."
  "Who?"
  "Boris Johnson. He's got himself a battlebus. And the best thing about it is, the thing was made in Germany and Poland. Now there's irony for you."
  "That's it started. It'll be lies from here on in. Best prepare for the onslaught."
  "From both sides, Ellis. Misinformation. As thick as snow on a roof."
  And she'd nailed it. There was misinformation from both sides … Personally speaking, when it came down to it, I favoured lies. I felt that better than misinformation. A bunch of fucking liars.
  They started immediately the bell rang.

The prime example was the spurious reports that money would flood back into the NHS if the leaver's campaign was successful. Free trade deals were on the cards, beginning with zero tariffs.

They must have taken us for simpletons with the crap they were spouting.

Two thirds of jobs in manufacturing are dependent on demand from the EU, and when Turkey joins, thousands of people will flock to the UK.

The list was endless. The fight turned dirty. We always knew it would.

For this vote we went down to the borders and stayed a week and a half.

The girls were glad to see us, as they always were, and us them. And reciprocating the hospitality shown them when up for the independence vote, gave them the chance to shine in the kitchen with not a carryout in sight.

"This time we're going for a home cooking theme. Eunice has been honing her skills."

"I wouldn't say, exactly, honing my skills. More like a polish up. And as we never did get the Chinese peppered beef from that menu, that's what we're having tonight. Remember that one, Jefferey?" she said. "The Chinese peppered beef? All home made. I looked up the recipe on my vast collection of food porn, and that's what we're having tonight. Chinese black peppered beef with medium egg noodles."

That was a thumbs up from Joyce and myself, and they served it with Tsingtao beer.

We sat till midnight conversing, then went to bed. The count wasn't to begin until nine the following morning and we wished to get a good night's sleep. It had been a long day, and an early rise was on the cards. We wanted to take it all in.

Breakfast was served at 8am and everyone tucked right in.

True to her word Eunice cooked up a feast, and we started with scrambled egg, bacon and fried tomato, served on a slice of home-baked, wholemeal cob; heavily buttered. This was followed by breakfast scones, peanut butter and jam. A pot of fresh-brew, arabica coffee or tea for those who preferred.

We sat ourselves down in the living room area to catch the results as they came. Then round about eleven at night, when we were still tucking into our Chicken Ceylon with chapati, Eunice had prepared earlier, we knew it was over and the leavers had won. It was a close run thing, coming in at 52 to 48% in their favour, and we were devastated. We were well aware, as things stood, this was only the beginning. It would perhaps take forever to hammer out a deal, then once they had, the fun would begin.

Cameron resigned as Prime Minister shortly after the announcement and Miriam said he was a gutless pig and better off out of it. "He'll lie low for a time then sneak back in through the back door. One of his cronies will give him a position and all will be forgiven. The public have short memories. After a while they forget things that happened and get on with their lives as before."

"Who'll be next, do you think?" asked Joyce, and do you think there will be a general election?"

"Knowing the Tories, I doubt there will be a general election. They'll pick someone from their ranks, and it will be business as before. Two or three will run for the job then an internal party election will take place to choose the winner. And that will be that. They're not about to hold an election they can't win. That would be seen as suicide."

Back in the Calders barely three weeks later the marionette arrived.

Theresa May. Who would have thunk it? What bag did they pull her from? A lucky one?

Her time wouldn't be long all the same. Brexit would bite her in the rear, and eventually leave her no other option than to resign. She lost the Commons majority after calling a general election in 2017, and never recovered. A boxer on the ropes standing up to a pummelling with time running out at speed.

Wooden and forced, her public persona was looked on as 'trying to be.' Even her colleagues had difficulty working out what she was thinking.

Ministerial resignations and parliamentary rebellions had no effect on her. She soaked them up like a sponge. Oblivious to mounting chaos around her, she told them "Nothing has changed."

It had.

She fell on her sword in 2019.

Next up, mad Liz Truss.

"Where will it end?" I asked Joyce. "It's as if it's one round of madness after another from the Tories. Blunder after blunder. They don't listen to anybody bar themselves. And they always think they're right. It's as if they're living on a planet in a different solar system from us. They're so far out of touch with what's happening in the country, they're running a different show. Either that or they don't care."

"Don't care. That's the way I see it. In it for themselves and close circle of rich friends. And don't forget the oligarchs. They'll be getting something in return for lining their coffers."

"I ask you ... Liz Truss? ... Who the hell is she?"

"A remain supporter," said Joyce, "who used to march against Thatcher when she was a Liberal Democrat activist. Opinionated as far as I know. Someone who likes to win, at all costs."

"That's all we need, another crazy in charge. Another one who hasn't a clue as to what's taking place."

Forty-five days she lasted in the post and managed to collapse the economy.

Roll up, roll up, for the Circus of Madness.

Enter the Master of Buffoonery

Next to have a go, and also unelected, the madcap Boris Johnson. Not a madcap in the usual sense. A madcap cover-up man. A bare faced liar who wouldn't know the truth if it stared him straight in the face. Like all the rest in the Tory party and politics in general.

pri-vi-leged

1

PRIVILEGED
PRIVILEGED
PRIVILEGED
PRIVILEGED

PRIVILEGED
PRIVILEGED
PRIVILEGED

PRIVILEGED to wipe
their ass on your face
then stick your head
in a tank.

PRIVILEGED to keep
you stuck in your place
you got no money
in the bank.

PRIVILEGED to say
it was not me
then watch as it
all goes clank.

PRIVILEGED to sneer
they make it quite clear
they would smile
as they twisted the shank.

2

They SQUIRM and wriggle
at every turn
like fish on the end of a hook.
Then thumb their nose
and say "Fuck you"
whilst drawing an arrogant look.

They certainly wouldn't
PISS on you
supposing you were on fire.
You haven't got time
for that sort of thing
when studying the art of a LIAR.

3

They lie to your face
they lie to the press
they lie on tv too.

They lie to the old
they lie to the young
they lie to me and you.

They lie with every breath they take
it's jam on a fireman's pole.
It's time we rammed a stick
of HERCULES dynamite up their hole.

HOLE!

*It's time we rammed a stick
of HERCULES dynamite up their hole.*

One debacle after another. A giant Whac-A-Mole. We were now in recession and if Boris had a mind to sort things out, he'd another think coming. They'd dropped us in it when the vote went in their favour to leave the EU, and there was no going back. They'd burnt their bridges, and all the crying over spilt milk was useless.

He was there to get things done, all the same. And if he acted the fool, good and well. He was seen as the man for the job by those that knew him, and it made no difference to them he'd compared women wearing burqas and niqabs to letter boxes or hid in a fridge to avoid reporters attempting to interview him on the eve of the 2019 general election. That didn't matter. Nor did claiming the Libyan city of Sirte would have a bright future as a holiday resort once investors cleared the bodies away. He'd a million like that and pressed them.

Liverpool wallowing in victim status.

Don't mention the war.

In the meantime, he was next in line to come through the revolving door.

Nine month later Joyce was dead, and I was living on my own.

*

BOOK FIVE

*

The Lord shall smite thee with a consumption, and with a fever, and with an inflammation, and with an extreme burning, and with the sword, and with blasting, and with mildew; and they shall pursue thee until thou perish.
                              Deuteronomy 28:22

1

I was devastated. I never expected it would end like this, though I don't suppose I'm alone. Bodies were piling up for a slot to be burnt in the local crematorium. And this was the story across the country.

The government had put us in lockdown.

I don't know how it came about, or even how we caught it, but we ended up with Covid 19 and Joyce went downhill fast. I had to call an ambulance, and that was the last I saw her.

They took her away to the ICU where she died a horrible death. Hooked up to a machine, trying to keep her alive. Which in the end was farce in itself, as they didn't even know what it was; Stabbing in the dark and groping about at a thing they didn't understand. And as I was infected, attending her funeral was strictly out of the question. I was confined and told to stay home under threat of a heavy fine. I was contaminated.

My mind was in knots and the images in my head took on a life of their own:

A chunk of ice the size of a hockey puck floated downstream in the direction of the weir. It was a difficult sensation to describe, but best if I give it a go for the record and clarify how it felt.

Winter ice is one thing, and as I scribbled notes - mostly unintelligible - in a small pocket notepad I noticed the smaller of the letters appeared to rearranged themselves into something more intelligible, as if trying to communicate happiness. But I knew this was weird, as happiness was the last thing on my mind, and would be for a while. Envisaging happiness was as far removed as any expectation I had of winning the lottery. It wasn't about to happen.

That's when the jeering began.

It sounded as if it were coming from overhead and grew in intensity the closer I got to a set of headlights out on the jetty. Maybe it was aliens trying to make human contact, but as I didn't believe in aliens, I quickly dispelled that notion, deciding it was more than likely a couple of teenage lovers making out on the back seat of a Ford Fiesta, and quickly turned back to the road.

Death comes for a crocodile. A pack of Arctic wolves.

As part of the government strategy to keep things under control they started to brew their own.

It was at this point the wheels came off altogether and I was thrown twenty feet in the air, coming down, heavily, in a ditch by the side of the road. Targets had been thrown up and people took pop shots, unbeknown I was there. I quickly raised the flag of surrender. They grabbed me and dragged me out.

"We've been looking for you," said the one with the stripes. "Did you think you could slip the net? Once we've got you there's no escape. The only way out is death."

I was on my own and legislation didn't make provision for the ill.

They took me back and strapped a full-face respirator to my head.

It grew dark.

A thick sediment settled around me, and I couldn't move. I felt I was being sucked under.

"Celebrity energy is very powerful. Don't stop liking me."

The ice went over the weir as water. I switched on the washing machine.

The Heart Sutra helped, and in the intervening weeks, I studied hard in an attempt to get a handle on it. I felt it would help in my mourning of Joyce, and would, had she been alive, brought a smile to her face.

"Told you so. It wasn't that difficult; once you got your head round things. "

I started to sit shikantaza, every day at twelve.

It was an arduous undertaking, and one I found demanding.

You'd think nothing would be easier than sitting still for forty minutes, letting the thoughts run riot in your head, knowing it comes down to the subtle activity of allowing things to be completely at rest, just as they are, and to hell with the workings of the world. Not so. It takes practice. Your body aches in places, aches in places, your body aches. Knees and lower back numb.

I'd sit like this for the allotted time then read the sutra for an hour.

And I was getting there. It was beginning to make sense; most of the time. Then it wouldn't make sense. Then it'd make sense. Then it wouldn't make sense again. Every time I considered I was making headway, it confused me again. I could see light in the distance. All I had to do was stick with it.

As Joyce explained: Emptiness; a total lack of self existence, I got it. What did I see when I looked at the wooden table in front of me? Everything. The seed, the tree etc. Nothing is born or dies. existent or non-existent. Things are always in a state of becoming. This is because that is. This is not because that is not. Dependant origination. Things just are. There only is. Neither one thing nor another. Things as they are. Nonduality.

Here Shariputra,
form is Emptiness, Emptiness is form.
Form is not separate from Emptiness,
Emptiness is not separate from form.
Whatever is form is Emptiness,
whatever is Emptiness is form.
The same holds for sensation, perception,
volition and consciousness.
Here, Shariputra, all dharmas are marked by Emptiness,
not by purity or impurity, increase or decrease,
birth or annihilation.

2

Even after a review of lockdown when some of the restrictions were lifted and people were once again allowed to leave their homes with the recommendation they wear a face mask in public places such as shops and public transport, I remained inside. I was terrified. Terrified of catching it again and ending up like Joyce. The prospect of being thrown in an oven with neither family nor friends in attendance to say their last goodbyes was mind-numbing. I'd rather stay in lockdown till all was done and dusted, and the threat of Covid eliminated. Or at the least, a vaccine was available that would allow us some degree of immunity.

Staying indoors in the meantime held no fear for me. My fear lay beyond the walls in what was in the air outside.

I had everything I needed here; Joyce had seen to that.

It was as if she knew what was coming and had spent the last however many years preparing for such an event. It was uncanny. And the stock she'd accumulated would have kept a family of four from starvation for well over a year. So, in that respect I was set without the need for worry. There was enough there to live it up on a daily basis without the need to repeat. I could mix and match, chop and change, different meals every day.

Breakfast, lunch, and dinner sorted; nothing to worry about.

Yet I missed Joyce. There was no getting away from the fact I missed her. I loved her, and to have had her wrenched away in the manner she was, left me sort of crippled. We hadn't spent much time apart since getting together in the first place. Now I was living on my own and could feel it. Memories were all I had. Beautiful memories all the same. Memories that made me smile.

I prepared a plate of keema matar from a tin of mince, a tin of peas, dried onion, dried garlic, a couple of spoonful of Madras masala, and a handful of dried coriander.

I sat with a spoon in little India, thinking of our times abroad.

I wondered if Lena was still alive or if she'd gone the way of Jules and dropped dead. Not necessarily on a trip somewhere; rather in her home whilst writing then lights out. Or perhaps she'd gone the way of Joyce. It was a possibility, what with it being a pandemic. It wasn't selective. There was a chance David and Rosa had also gone the same way. I couldn't tell, and I didn't know. We'd somehow lost contact.

The girls were fine, I knew that. We'd stayed in touch. And when I'd called them to let them know the situation with Joyce and what was happening they were distraught. They couldn't believe it, especially the fact I wasn't permitted to attend her funeral due to being infected myself. They said if they could, and the law had permitted, they'd have been up in a flash. I knew that. I knew I could count on the girls for support. All I had to do was ask.

Then I got back to that wooden table: It set me to thinking again:

Generations of ancestors. A man eats breakfast. A chicken, a cow, and a pig. The clothing industry, slave labour, container ships, and ports.

I thought of the sun, the clouds, the rain. A truck and all that involved. There was the glass to consider, along with the tyres. The wipers, the foam in the seats. Every bolt, rivet and nut suddenly to come into the equation. Ropes and straps; the steering wheel. Lights, reflectors, and mirrors. Everything you could think of that made up the truck and everything that made up that. The list was endless, and the more I brought it to mind the more I got a grip on Emptiness.

There was the chainsaw to think about, and all that involved. Cogs and screw and plastic and oil and drilling rigs and chains. The North sea, the drilling platform, workers and breakfasts again. Helicopters and pilots.

I could have contemplated forever and never got to the end. The tree, the sawmill, the bricks, the sand, the seashells, the roads, the carpenter. Then there was the shopping mall and builders of such. Tiles and marble and slate.

I hardly had started when I smiled to myself: Dependent Origination.

The noble Avalokiteshvara bodhisattva,

whilst   practicing   the   deep   practice   of prajnaparamita
looked upon the five Skandhas
and seeing they were empty of self-existence said …

Now I was getting somewhere. You couldn't simply go and find yourself a beautiful wooden table.
"Now we're getting our head round it Joyce." I said as I looked at her urn.

That evening I made congee and topped it off with Lap Cheong and a healthy portion of kimchi I was lucky enough to have Joyce lay down six weeks prior to her death. She'd made five kilo of the stuff on request, and as kimchi went it was the best I'd tasted. Leaving it in its jars, in a cool environment, I suspected it would last a year. Perhaps a little bit longer if lucky, if I didn't eat the lot before hand. I gave it a year at the longest point. I didn't want to push my luck. Giving it longer than that, I supposed, was likely out of the question.

I circled the words on a calendar entry for May of the year 21: KIMCHI'S END.

Nighttime was a nightmare. I always woke, from the little sleep I did manage to get, with the sweats and fear, having dreamt of Joyce's demise. It wasn't pretty. I was tied to a chair at the bottom of her bed and forced to watch as she died. Put in a coma then intubated before being attached to a ventilator, then gasping back to life. Eventually compelled to turn her off, when those with the power and full-face covid masks decided that that was that.

Untied then forced at the point of a bayonet to flick the switch to the red.

I'd turn then discover she wasn't beside me then sit on the edge of the bed.

I was at my wits end and tried everything to get a decent night's sleep. Nothing worked. Neither alcohol, herbal teas, prescription drugs or otherwise. Every night the same routine, the same damn hellish dreams. Daylight never arrived quick enough. Then brought along problems of its own.

I found it impossible to concentrate on anything, apart from zen, for more than a minute or so at a time. The zen thing was different, as it brought me closer to Joyce in a weird way. It was as if, when reading the Heart Sutra or thinking on Emptiness, she was there in the room beside me. It gave me solace and I'd work on it a while, feeling that it gave me strength. I was exhausted and had a constant headache. Every bone in my body felt crushed and my muscles were severely fatigued. I was short tempered - though only had myself to live with - and my heart palpitations were off the chart. I was breathless and plagued with terrible tinnitus. Diarrhoea and stomach pain. Depression and fog on the brain a bitch. Other than that, I was fine.

The news of Cummings' trip on the telly almost drove me over the edge.

Who the hell did this joker think he was? Infected people had been told to self-isolate and here he was swanning off with his family to County Durham to stay at a house on his parents' land. He even had the nerve to say he had acted responsibly when question by reporters. What the fuck? Was it one rule for us and another for them? I was livid. Here was Joyce dead and gone and myself confined to quarters. It wasn't responsible they didn't heed their own advice.

I'd watch this lot with a careful eye in the following weeks and months.

I prepared a chana masala, then made a chapati using wholewheat Elephant atta, Joyce had got at the halal store. I set it to the side then called the girls for a chat on Facebook Messenger; as techie as I managed to get.

It was now the only contact I had with the outside; barring the news on television. I was living an insular life of my own making and had vowed, all going well, to remain indoors until covid ran its course or a suitable vaccine was rolled out and a sense of normality returned, however long it took.

Abiding by the rules and staying home, quite unlike Mr Cummings.

Nighttime came and I kept myself up by reading Papillon.

My thinking on that one was that by keeping myself awake during the hours of darkness, sleep would come a whole lot easier if I lay on the couch and closed my eyes as afternoon approached. Wrong. What a mistake that was. Not only did I not escape the horrid dreams that had beset me and catch up on much needed sleep as was my intention, they intensified. It was horror piled upon horror, and after five days of this I returned to my old routine of trying to sleep at night. I was trapped, and all there was for it was to face up to the fact. Trapped like a bear, in a snare in the woods, with no one to help. And supposing there had been. I didn't see a solution. Others in the same boat must have felt the same; trapped with no way out.

They rolled out a vaccine on the 8th of December, The Feast of the Immaculate Conception.

Cultural festivities
processions and food.
Fireworks, masses and parades.

3

It was snowing outside, and as I breakfasted on a plate of porridge and tinned pears The Biscuit Factory sprang up on the telly on the Scottish news at half past six. It was still there, operating as it always had, churning out Jammie Dodgers and Wagon Wheels by the truck load. It had taken a knock when members of staff tested positive for covid, although for the time being, according to a statement issued by senior management they had no plans to close the facility; Business as usual, they'd said.

I was surprised by this, as I didn't expect the place to be there any longer never mind still operational.

I laughed to myself then my mind harked back to my time there long ago.

Maggie whose husband was on longer than a dumpling when he started. That one really shook me up. I hadn't heard it before and remembered choking on what I was eating, spraying it all over the table. Carol and Lynn. Agnes' man ... he was all mouth and trousers. Vera ... Vera's other half who was done before the starting pistol went off then spent the remainder of the night in a state of bat torpor.

Where were they now? Were they still alive? If so, they'd be in their nineties.

I put them down as long since gone. Dead and buried to a woman.

I took myself to Little India. Sat shikantaza.

I was beginning to feel better about the zen thing; smug even. Then I remembered a word from Joyce. Don't. It was a big mistake, she said, and one often made by people thinking they've finally got it after months or years of struggle. They think they've had a eureka moment and smugness sets in. Don't. For everyone who gets it a million don't, and somehow think they have. Big mistake. Not two: One. A little realization is a dangerous thing. You tie yourself up instead of becoming liberated.

I had to dial it back somewhat to avoid falling into the trap.

Christmas 2020 was grand, and the party I threw lasted three days, by the end of which I was buggered and in need of rest.

As host I took responsibility for food, drink, and entertainment, along with dressing the table, putting up the tree, and hanging decorations. All was well, the day in question going off without a hitch.

I started by pulling a cracker with myself; donned the little, plastic moustache, put on the purple paper crown. Laughed at the corny joke.

I drank two glass of cheap champagne, went out and killed a chicken.

Hats of to gran. Her proviso concerning the chickens had always been a great source of fresh eggs, along with the occasional bird. More so now than ever.

I noticed a tyre on the Fiat was flat and I didn't have a spare. I wasn't going anywhere so wasn't unduly worried. I gave it a kick as I passed with the chicken. Swore underneath my breath.

I opened a bottle of port midday then dressed the chicken for the pot. I placed it in a Dutch oven along with carrots and stock, then set it to the side. I poured two tins of potatoes into a baking tray, added salt, crushed black pepper, sprayed them with butter oil. A tin of sprouts I tipped in a pot along with a tin of peas. I'd think about dessert closer to the time. I lit a little cigar.

Things didn't get better than this, and the only thing that could have topped it and took it to another level was Joyce being here; giving me instructions as to timings for chicken and how best to crisp-up potatoes. But she wasn't, and I didn't suspect she'd be happy if she'd an idea I was sitting moping her absence with a long face, feeling sorry for myself at Christmas, or any other time. She wouldn't. So, with that in mind I poured a port and opened a can of stout.

tele, film, music/dance.
tele, film, music.
tele, film, music/dance.
dance, dance, dance.

I slung the chook in the oven at two … Ready to eat by four.

And eat I did; with relish … I started with Baxters minestrone before sitting down to the main.

I'd made a sage and onion stuffing with PAXO, and served up with cranberry sauce it was a treat. A Christmas dinner fit for a king. Fit for me. I took my time, enjoying every mouthful, as I sat at the table contemplating my surroundings, and blessing the day I first met Joyce, Christmas In The Heart, played in the background, adding a beautiful ambiance to proceedings, warming up the room. I lighted candles then pulled the curtains, they flickered and danced in the dark.

I filled a glass with warm wine. Let the first and main go down, went to the cellar for dessert.

The choice was endless, and as I scoped the rows of cans, arranged by Joyce into their respective content - beans/legumes, meats, tomatoes, fruit, desserts etc - I finally went for a tin of lychees and a tin of tapioca.

tele, film, music/dance.
tele, film, music.
tele, film, music/dance.
dance, dance, dance.

I slept intermittently, as best I could on the sofa, but the dreams continued to come.

Boxing day I boiled two eggs for breakfast, stripped what was left of the chicken from the bone, made myself a Madras.

Drink.
tele, film music/dance.
tele, film, music.
tele, film, music/dance.
dance, dance, dance.

The third day was a blur due to my alcohol intake and when I came to on the floor on the fourth, I'd had enough. I wasn't getting any younger and my body told me that. The mind may have been willing, but as for the body … that was a different story. I was about ready for the knacker's yard and was well aware another bout of covid would likely kill me off or leave me long-term suffering.

    I wasn't for taking either onboard. I kept myself indoor.

4

Traitors and stabbers in the back abound as State collaboration in the miscarriage of justice impacts the publics perception of events that have taken place.

"Considering the evidence and renewed scrutiny with which it has been examined I feel I have no option other than place it before the Guilt Society, recently recovered from the wastebasket."

"Here, here."

"Silence in court."

The Speaker calls for order.

"Not all conspirators are members of the Club your Lordship. There were those who arrived solely for cake."

"Cake?"

"Cake and booze, as far as I'm aware ... A little dancing on the side."

The Judge looked over his rimless specs. "Blood at Pompey's feet?"

"Only if they push for abdication and cause him to fall on his sword."

"It won't take a sheep's liver to divine the outcome of this debacle, or any animal's entrails. On the contrary. Once he's gone replace the head, it's always worked in the past. Always has and always will. Chop it off with a pugio."

Some were quaking in their boots at this, others didn't give a fig.

Christmas was restored by Charles II. A few took things to extremes.

*
BOOK SIX
*

A massive thaw is exposing traces of all of last years lies.

1

And there was me thinking no one threw a Christmas party on the scale of the one I held in the Calders last year. Wrong. The bastards from the Tory party had been living it up all along and taking us all for mugs.

Christmas party, leaving parties, drinks, nibbles, and games. They even had the nerve to label their Christmas do a cheese and wine night. Then once summer came round, and the sun appeared, send an email to one and all in order the cunts make hay:

'Socially distanced drinks.'

Hi all, after what has been an incredibly busy period, we thought it would be nice to make the most of the lovely weather and have some socially distanced drinks in the No 10 garden this evening. Please join us from 6pm and bring your own booze!

These people were living it up while we dropped dead like flies.

Social drinks at the end of the week, known as wine time Friday.

Social?

This was the most unsocially distanced party in the whole of the UK.

These bastards were at it. No 10 was a hotbed of iniquity with the Devil himself in charge. Social distancing didn't exist, and the wearing of face masks laughed at.

We're the ones in charge of the country, the peasants will do as they're told. Whip them into shape with fines and jail-time if necessary. That'll sort them out.

There was no national mourning for Phil either. In fact, it was alleged that on the eve of his funeral, staff at an 'event' were having sex. Banging each other in toilets and cupboards. Arses on copy machines.

These bastards have no respect for the common man.

The more that came out the angrier I got, and more came out each day. It didn't look as if it was about to end anytime soon, what with accusation after accusation each time I switched on the news or turned on the radio. These were people who were supposed to lead by example and show us all the way. Show us how it should be done and follow the letter of the law. Here they were in their Downing Street bubble, cocking a snook of distain.

This was the point I knew for sure I was done with politics for good.

Partygate.

I sat in Victorian bathing suit
as I flopped my floppy disk.
I'll never develop a film again
or look up a phone book list.

I'll never be back in the jungle
with Walkman or Betamax.
No sooner are things invented

than you have to put up with the cracks.

2

The next humans, I surmise, will be nothing like us. More AI than flesh and bone. The first step toward the expansion of a potential as yet unmined, hanging on ultraviolet markings, nectar at the centre of flowers.

"We didn't grow up with mustard," said George. "And jam was out of the question."

Apologies wouldn't be cutting it here, they'd learned to walk on two legs.

They published the book to a fanfare of plaudits in 1785. It was strange.

It was pathogen-depleted and untitled on the cover, but we all knew who it was by. We'd seen it all before with, Blonde on Blonde, Nashville Skyline, and Self Portrait. It was nothing new, and there was every likelihood we'd see it again when the opportunity presented.

"People get hung up on this stuff, when in actual fact the correct course of action is a shot of vitamin D."

Cumbersome protocols put in place to catch a thief in the night.

Alice had had enough. She pulled a gun from the bottom of her bag then shot herself in the head.

There are no honest politicians. We have entered a frightening new.

3

We eventually got the all clear on the 21 March 2022, and after confining myself to quarters for the best part of two year, I dreaded venturing out. I feared I'd developed agoraphobia during the course of my self-imprisonment, and the idea I'd have to take myself to town was not relished. On the contrary, it filled me with dread.

I'd grown to love my own space, along with my own company, and become accustomed to it. Enjoyed it even. So, the thought of standing in line in order to catch a bus - undoubtedly full of strangers - that would take me to town, didn't elicit any joy. Leaving home in the first instance: panic. The shopping centre, hell. But needs must.

I'd all but depleted the prepper-room stock and needed to resupply. On the last count I was down to five tins of Spanish sardines, three tins of butter beans, one bag of dried macaroni, a bottle of oil, two jars of strawberry jam, a jar of English mustard, six tins of chopped tomatoes, four tins of meatballs in gravy, a jar of pickle, a tin of goblin burgers, three tins of PEK chopped pork, A jar of hot dogs, a jar of beans (Polish), passata, and a Fray Bentos pie.

Now was the time to leave the house, if ever I was leaving at all.

But how?

I needed to devise a plan that'd get me out and about.

I'd been in the garden on an almost daily basis, collecting eggs and feeding the chickens. Picking herbs and veg. But this was different, and the longer I spent within the plot the less I felt a necessity to journey beyond its boundary. Why would I? Beyond the wall lay death. I was certain of that. And equally certain that assumption made no sense. I had to give myself a shake and accept the pandemic was over and get myself back out there. Back to the land of the living.

I made up my mind to go on Friday, a couple of days away.

In the meantime, I worried about the transport situation and was cognizant it was having to travel with others in a confined space that troubled me, and that alone. If I'd taken better care of the car, as I had the bike when I owned it, things would be different. I hadn't. I hadn't so much as looked at the thing since the start of covid, and it was this lack of action and care toward it that led to the predicament I found myself in. A flat tyre with no pump and a spare that was flat as well. There was nothing else for it. All I could do was bite the bullet and jump on the bus with the others. People like myself that were going about their business, hoping they'd return covid free. After a day at the office or wherever, just to return covid free.

I was worried. My mind a Guernica of twisted thoughts.

Worried beyond the normal state of what worried should normally be.

I messaged the girls on Facebook.

"Eunice, I don't know what to do," I said. "Maybe you can help?"

"Of course," she said, as Miriam came in to view and took a seat. "What can we do for you?"

"It's this whole covid thing," I said, I don't know what to do?"

"What do you mean?" said Miriam, pouring a glass of wine.

"I don't know what to do about going out … I know it's over and we've had the all clear from the government, but I'm worried. I'm worried I'll end up like Joyce, dumped in the back of a truck waiting to be burned, then no one there when it happens."

"That's crazy thinking," said Miriam. "You need to get it out of your head. It's over, Jeff. And besides, we've all been inoculated, so everybody's safe. So long as you've had the jabs you'll be fine."

"But that's just it," I said. "I haven't had any jags. I refused to get them as it involved leaving the house and I wasn't up for that. I didn't go out for fear of getting infected and am still of the same frame of mind. It terrifies me to think of it. Out there catching covid when I could have stayed home. Just my luck to catch the thing, once they said it was safe. If I thought we could bypass it, I'd gladly go back to Thatcher."

"Don't be silly," said Eunice. "I don't think Joyce would want you sitting about the house for fear of going out? Do you?"

I considered this in a rational way, then came to a rational conclusion.

I knew the girls were right, and the chances of me catching it at this stage were slim. With or without the jags. Things had cooled sufficiently they said to take myself on a trip.

"Into town," were Eunice's words. "Get your shopping and whatever you need. Then once you've done that go to a café for coffee and a slice of cake. You'll feel much better once you get home and know it's now safe to go out."

I thanked them then we spoke of the good times we'd had over the years.

I felt much better after that.

I still couldn't sleep.

I planned to get the bus at eight thirty, do my shopping as quick as possible, home for around midday. I was up at six and already my anxiety was building. I felt like a pressure cooker about to blow, and the heart palpitations were a worry. The coffee I drank didn't help. I should have known better. It was always the same when I drank coffee no matter the circumstances. And the cigarettes on top of that were adding fuel to the fire.

I could have stayed home where I felt safe, wrapped in my own cocoon. A safety net. At this point I was questioning whether I would have ventured out in a medical emergency. Finger hanging off: A plaster?

I had to do as the girl's said and get my head in order. The pandemic was over. People were moving on, and I had to do likewise. Worrying about it wasn't helping. The exact opposite. I had to change my mindset. I knew it. Get myself out onto the street.

I put on shoes, a jacket, a hat. Locked the door at my back.

Once outside things really went to shit, but I made it to the request stop.

The bus couldn't come quick enough. I wanted this over as soon as possible, and if it didn't come within the next five minutes I'd a mind to return home and to hell with the shopping. Fuck it. Go home and starve and that would be the end of it. No more torturing myself with head-shit I had no control over. Back in the Alya-vijnana, if I'd worked things out correctly. It seemed like a better choice.

Then the bus came. My heart sank. The thing was packed to the gunwales.

My sums were off. I'd calculated that by catching it at eight thirty I'd miss the rush. The workforce gone on the eight o'clock transit, starting around half past. They were. And as I took my seat, squashed in at the back, the claustrophobia began.

I was sweating profusely, brought about by the thought that if anything happened escape may be damn near impossible, given the number of souls crammed together in the vehicle. I had chronic chest pains and a mad fear the nausea I was feeling would, at any moment, manifest itself in full-blown projectile vomiting, covering the occupants, head to toe, in puke. I felt I was choking as the trembling began.

Who were these people? Then it dawned: students on their way to college.

My mind went, instantly, back to the 70s and what I was thinking of then. Nothing of any importance really, I was just being part of the game. I was young, and with youth my idea of what was important was far removed from what is important with the coming of age and responsibility. A nonsense.

I wished to shout.

I wished to tell the students to start thinking for themselves and get off the bus before it was too late. But decorum forbade. I wanted to let them know that once they entered into that contract there was no escape, next stop the mines. Escape while you can, for once the man gets you firmly in his grasp there is nothing you can do but scream. Scream till the end of days when you're sitting there drooling in an old folks home, thinking to yourself what a goddam waste of a life that could have been lived.

The bus pulled into the terminus then emptied. I decided I wasn't getting off.

I paid the return then went back home. Sat some shikantaza.

Dr Hook's, Jungle to the Zoo,
plays out over the credits.

*Special thanks
to
Lewis Carroll, Jonathan Swift,
Robert Louis Stevenson
Charles Baudelaire
Tristan Tzara
&
Robert Burns,
for their posthumous contributions.

graham greig
Off-Piste Manifesto 2024

As the Off-Piste skier is want to take the risk of being swept off the slope by Avalanche at any given moment, then so it is with the Off-Piste writer, poet or musician, in as much as the Avalanche is self-triggered by either shelling, howitzer, recoilless rifle or fuel-air explosive. The means is immaterial, as all that is of importance is that the Avalanche is triggered whenever the need felt.

Suffering and the end
of suffering
suffering and the end
of suffering
suffering and the end
of suffering
Ad Infinitum

As all periods of calm are invariably followed by crushing bouts of anxiety the Avalanche must always hit in the wake of comprehensible text or music score.

Who in their right mind shouts , : ! . (only to climb inside a box and die of slow inertia then come to the conclusion there is no IS better than was and what are to come?

By going Off-Piste you swear allegiance to bring the Avalanche down on the Reader/Listener at any time without prior warning, a barrage of the seemingly unintelligible. The Violence and Velocity of which must always force the Reader/Listener to take note:

We do not have a water cooler.
Football, football, football.
We do not have a water cooler.
Let the buggers choke.

We do not have a water cooler.
Football, football, football.
We do not have a water cooler.
Cowboys all but broke.

We do not have a water cooler.
Cooler, cooler, cooler.
We do not have a water cooler.
Poke, poke, poke.

Saturday morning six a.m.
        hung on the end of a rope.

This Avalanche, in whichever form it takes, must be constructed in a manner that mirrors the function of the Koan: intensely forcing the Reader/Listener to contemplate its meaning then ultimately - after an unspecified period of time - break through to understanding its place within the text/score itself. Though arriving at said breakthrough, each individual's interpretation will differ greatly from another's and ultimately render the Koan function non-existent.

After secreting a chalky substance that floated to the surface and donating eggs that were found to be inedible by all, save certain members of a lost tribe from the Amazon rainforest, I determined to bring the Incubator of Violence into play, then watch as it took its toll.

The Avalanche text/score may baffle, or indeed seem impenetrable to most, while always making sense on the subconscious level, each word or phrase taking one in a new direction then back to the text/score proper.
   Think, don't think. Think, don't think. Think, don't think. Don't think. Non-thought the appropriate mind-set when hit by Avalanche.

The positioning of Avalanche is of little importance, though some thought is necessary.
   Avalanche may be inserted either at the beginning of a text/score. The end of a text/score, or incorporated within the body of the text/score itself. This will be determined by the writer's/musician's own discretion. Where poetry is concerned an individual poem may consist entirely of Avalanche.

Sources to be considered when applying Avalanche within a work of literature are as follows:
Newspaper/magazine articles (cut-up).
National Geographic Magazine (cut-up, of special interest).
The Bible (cut-up).
Stream of consciousness technique.

Books that have entered the public domain/Contextual reassignment.

The text/score may be amended or updated at any point post production.

Music may be cut using the various audio trimmers available.

All work must be self edited/produced in order it maintains its integrity.

AI is NOT an option under any circumstances.

Off-Piste is whatever the writer/musician wishes it to be, striking at any moment with a deadly force as the Off-Piste artist negotiates his way downhill at great personal risk, ignoring any and all warning signs that at any second Avalanche may strike.

Off-Piste is CLICK on first page you intend to remove number from.

Off-Piste is BREAK from continuous …

Off-Piste is TEXT page.

Off-Piste is HEADER & FOOTER.

Off-Piste is previous writing CLICK to unlink then repeat.

Off-Piste is base jumping, diving with sharks and eating soup with chopsticks.

Off-Piste is self publishing to the detriment of income.

Off-Piste is alive and well wherever the artist lurks.

Off-Piste is.

I have taken it upon myself to write this manifesto in direct response to the mind-numbing banality and repetition of the formulaic detective novel, fantasy novel, romance novel, etc. And to the numerous musical acts who, in their great wisdom, foist the self-same album on the general public time after time, without recourse to a refund.

it's the only way to ski.

Printed in Great Britain
by Amazon